FOOLISH HEROINES

June Wentland is an ordinary woman who believes that extraordinary things can happen if you keep your eyes peeled and your heart open to new possibilities. She grew up in Hull, moving to Manchester and Bristol before settling in Wiltshire. June has worked in community development and outreach for libraries as well as being a rather lacklustre waitress and on an assembly line sticking tassels onto lampshades.

She has had stories televised and published by the BBC and her poetry has appeared in many literary journals and anthologies. This is her first novel.

Foolish Heroines

JUNE WENTLAND

Valley Press

First published in 2021 by Valley Press
Woodend, The Crescent, Scarborough, YO11 2PW
www.valleypressuk.com

ISBN 978-1-912436-63-7
Cat. no. VP0184

A CIP record for this book is available from the British Library.

Cover and text design by Peter Barnfather.
Edited by Jo Haywood.

Printed and bound in Great Britain by
Imprint Digital, Upton Pyne, Exeter.

*For all my family – to those who've gone before,
those who'll follow and those who are alive and kicking.*

*I hope Nick, Louise, James, Niamh, Jamie,
Daniel and Leo won't mind a special mention.*

I

When Janina Reston touched Owen Reston's arm and her hand passed straight through it, it only confirmed what she'd suspected for some time – her partner was simply a figment of her imagination. He wasn't really there at all. She wondered if he'd ever been real and, if so, whether he'd disappeared all in one go or whether it had happened gradually, bit by bit.

She had an acquaintance whose husband had vanished in the supermarket. One minute he was walking down the aisle between the cream crackers and the packs of lager, and the next he was gone. He'd undressed, leaving his clothes and shoes in a neat pile. Then he'd dived into the salty depths of a deep freezer amongst the battered cod and the new crabmeat fish cakes, never to be seen again, tossed about for infinity on the tides of consumer capitalism. Missing, presumed dead.

Owen had been looking increasingly transparent since the jumper incident. The question was, who'd put the jumper on to boil wash? Who'd committed the sin? *Wash with care in cool water*, the label said, delicate. A sure candidate for programme J: *suitable for hand wash items with a crease guard and a gentle spin*.

The jumper had hung from her hand like an unexpected blossom, an out of season bloom, defying horticulturalist theory. It emitted an aura of novelty, a self-conscious exclamation mark at its own existence. Perfectly circular drops of water clung to the surface, resisting its pull but inevitably absorbed by it.

"What the fuck's that?" Owen asked as he and Janina stood in the kitchen. "Is it my jumper?"

Janina leaned against the sink and weighed up the possibilities, the jumper still hanging from her hand like a question for which a solution must be found.

When objects, or people for that matter, went through such drastic change could they really still claim to be what they'd originally been? How many married individuals were still the same people they'd been on their wedding day? Did that annul the marriage? Janina and Owen stared at the offending piece of laundry, still steaming from the hot wash. Neither could quite draw their eyes away from it.

"Do you want it to be?" she asked. It was a philosophical question but he took it as an insensitive reply.

"What do you think?" he said.

"I think you put it in with the fast colours." she said. "Or it could have got put on with the boil wash."

The impasse couldn't go on forever in such a small kitchen, so Janina walked out into the garden. A few birds sang in the newly blossoming trees, pinprick specks of delicate colour, gently piercing the cool air; the trees' roots like wooden toes entwined affectionately or engaged in a hidden power struggle beneath the grass. Concealed beneath Janina and Owen's conversation had been the unsaid implication that, somewhere along the line, she was to blame for the jumper. As if, at some point, she'd been duped into signing a contract with unreadably small print that made her responsible for any shrinkages or mishaps that took place within the womb-like confines of the washing machine. Any mistake would be viewed as collusion between woman and technological hardware.

She draped the jumper over her shoulder while she

pegged out the other washing on the old rotary clothesline. Her daughters, Lidka and Eve, were playing a square-less game of hopscotch on the overgrown triangle of lawn at the side of the shed.

In each small city garden, clean washing flapped a circular journey to nowhere. Each garment hung, expertly positioned, to optimally exploit the breeze – pegged to perfection. The jumper struck an incongruous note of error, swinging and clinging in its carefree way.

How had she come to be standing here on such a sunny Sunday afternoon? Once she'd been a schoolgirl choosing positions carefully – attempting to work out the rules like a complicated knitting pattern. She tried to learn the abbreviations for what society said was right – pleasure through tact not tactile delight. There were a few men for whom she'd almost learnt the womanly crafts. She would have taken rich ripe fruits and stirred them to a syrup in heavy saucepans until, with her own magic, she altered the state of the fruits into a globulus, sticky, sticky, sweet, sweet jam. A domestic quickstep of fulfilled desire. She would have learnt the ancient skill of darning, divesting the passage of time with a perpetual state of newness, and smoothing the wrinkles out of hours with calm, competent hands. If they'd tired of her she would have taken the attributes of other women and painfully appliquéd them in neat suppliant stitches to her own skin.

She could have become the sort of woman who actually puts whites in the white wash instead of everything on programme D, who makes custard from eggs and milk instead of ready-made cartons, and drinks strictly herbal tea. She'd baulked at all this but, somewhere along the way, she felt she'd compromised; abdicated responsibility for her own future. In a sense, she'd given away her soul. Now, here she was in her thirties without a soul.

Were souls circular too – like the drops of water on the jumper? A friend once told her about the increasing size of her cervical cap. She'd started with a small one at the age of eighteen and then, with progressive pregnancies expanding her cervical circumference, she'd ended up with one the size of a bowler hat. Did souls shrink in direct proportion to the expansion of cervical circumference? The circle of the cervix rubbing against the circle of the soul? The healthy red corpuscles pulsing round the rim and hollowness through the centre?

Oh, how aerodynamic some women would be if only they realised. What low air resistance they'd have. To what heights they'd be able to soar like self-powered frisbees – cutting sharply, economically, through the soft bloodless substance of other people's dreams.

A sudden gust of wind swept through the garden, grabbing at the newly formed blossoms and whipping at Janina's skirt. It almost pulled her off her feet as the jumper flapped joyously between a pair of grey socks and an off-white sheet.

2

"My wife doesn't understand me," Owen said, when he visited the doctor a few weeks later. Owen wasn't sure what made him utter such a statement when he'd really come about a sore throat. And especially when he knew, full well, that Dr Jelf was a personal friend of Janina's.

Ever since the jumper incident, Janina had been acting very strangely. She hardly engaged with him at all.

"If I'd had a dose of penicillin for each time one of my male patients told me that their wife didn't understand them," said Dr Jelf. "I'd be in big trouble if I contracted a rare tropical infection."

This remark was lost on Owen. Lots of Dr Jelf's remarks were lost on people, partly because of her obstinate fluency in Latin. She used it liberally in general conversation, otherwise the years she spent learning a dead language at school would have been wasted.

"She says I don't exist," said Owen.

"When did the symptoms start?" asked Dr Jelf.

"Since she shrank my jumper," said Owen. "Although when I think about it, she's always been a bit unusual."

"Not your wife," said Dr Jelf. "I mean you. Let me have a look at your tongue."

Owen was about to ask what his tongue had got to do with his wife's rather individual character traits but decided to comply instead. Celia Jelf peered at it in what Owen considered to be a censorial manner before dismissing it without thanking it for putting in an appearance or giving a verdict on its condition.

"Take these tablets three times a day," she said, scribbling a prescription and giving Owen a smile that was as inscrutable as her handwriting. "Maybe they'll make you a bit less blurry round the edges."

"Outrageous," said Owen as he headed for the door. He didn't have the energy to explain whether he was referring to Dr Jelf's comment or her appalling handwriting or both.

"It was a joke," said Celia Jelf.

"Illness is not a joking matter," said Owen.

"Tell me about it," said Celia.

Owen half closed the surgery door and then, a health and safety officer by profession and by inclination, he felt obliged to turn back into the room. He was staring at a pile of medical journals on a shelf above head height. It was an avalanche of cutting-edge medical theory ready to slice into a patient's head. He nodded towards it.

"An accident waiting to happen," was all he said.

Owen called in at the paper shop on his way home. He took a copy of *Mountaineering Today* from the tidily stocked shelf, which he noticed was well secured to the wall. In Owen's mind there wasn't anything incongruous about being a health and safety officer by day and a mountaineer in his spare time. Safety consciousness limited and contained the possibilities of danger in climbing whilst climbing pushed the limits of safety measures to their extremes.

When Owen reached home, a tidy end terrace house on the edge of the inner city, he carefully ascended a step ladder and checked the batteries in each of the four smoke alarms while he waited for the kettle to boil. Then he sat down with a cup of tea to look at pictures of unassailable peaks and to read about journeys through inhospitable terrain. The cats,

Gus and Carlotta, locked out and waiting for food, sat on the windowsill observing Owen through narrow eyes – blue as risk assessment forms, cold as mountain glaciers.

"How's that husband of yours?" Celia Jelf asked her old friend Janina, when she went to see her a few weeks later.

Dr Jelf had slightly reorganised her surgery. The medical journals were still in exactly the same position but she'd moved her consulting desk to the other side of the room to keep herself, and her patients, out of harm's way in case the predicted avalanche should occur.

"He doesn't exist," said Janina.

"He disagrees," said Dr Jelf.

"He's a product of my subconscious," said Janina. "He's someone I dreamt up."

"Janina," said Dr Jelf, a bit snappily – she'd had a hard day. "Your sub-conscious might have created a man who doesn't exist but Owen does. He has a heartbeat. I'm his GP; I can vouch for that."

"Objects, and people, can exist in some situations but cease to exist in others," said Janina. She was thinking of the undelivered parcel she'd waited at home for all day and which the courier insisted had been delivered. It may well have been deposited somewhere but it had never inhabited the space outside Janina's front door and therefore had no reality within the immediate vicinity of her home. It had been totally vexing. Now, here was Celia Jelf making the same sort of oversimplified assertion. It was all too much.

"You're a doctor of medicine not a doctor of philosophy," said Janina. "Everything is much more complicated than that. If you're going to take Owen's side in this, I'll take my germs elsewhere."

3

Having fallen out with Celia Jelf, Janina had to turn to other friends to mull over her problems. Since the jumper incident, Janina had acquired a friend called Gladys. Gladys was a spider. She lived in a web in the corner of the downstairs toilet, hidden in the shadow of the cistern. She was a large black spider and Janina often chatted to her.

Slowly as their one-sided conversations progressed, Janina decided that the spider was a reincarnation of her grand-mother. She decided she was wise and sympathetic and that she belonged to the species of spider that eats their partner after mating with them. Eventually, one day soon, after recovering memories from her past life she would speak in human tongue. For some unexplained reason hidden deep in Janina's own psyche, she believed her spider grandmother would speak with a pronounced Italian accent. Unfortunately, Gladys never got the chance to speak as, in a moment of misguided trust, Janina told Owen about her. And one day, in the middle of an argument, Owen flushed Gladys down the toilet.

Janina and Owen faced each other over the toilet bowl. Janina seized hold of the toilet brush, though neither of them was quite sure what she was planning to do with it.

"That was my grandmother you just drowned," said Janina.

"You took more notice of what that spider said than anything I say," said Owen.

"Really?" said Janina. "She hadn't said anything yet. Are you telling me you felt insecure because of a spider?"

"Don't be stupid," said Owen.

"You didn't have to drown her. You could have found something to talk to yourself," said Janina, before adding helpfully. "There're some maggots at the bottom of the dustbin."

"You're a sick woman," said Owen, noticing one of Janina's grandmother's legs – it must have fallen off in the scuffle – still trailing on the toilet seat. He used a bit of toilet paper to plop it into the water below.

The next day Owen felt guilty. He came home with flowers. They were a budget bouquet from Fatima's Blossom Tree, the florist's at the other end of the street. He left them lying on the kitchen table, which strongly displeased Janina. How could he just leave them there? She would not accept the flowers without being properly presented with them. After Owen went to bed, she carefully put the blooms in water. She was downstairs before him the following morning to take them back out again. She placed them exactly where they'd been. When Owen went to work, she put them in water again. She couldn't bear to see them die. But still, she carefully took them out of the water before he arrived home in the evening. She did this every day.

Four days passed. The sun rose and waned and the moon sent down its delicate magnetic light, dictating the patterns of the tides around the globe. Leaves fell silently in the garden of Janina's home. The ivy on the walls continued its microscopic advance, slowly sucking the lifeblood from the bricks.

Inside the house, the children and the cats played in the trenches of domestic warfare – avoiding a sniper here, jumping across mined areas in psychological no man's land there – like resigned villagers who have devised cunning techniques of survival on land appropriated long ago by alien superpowers.

"If you can't be bothered to put those flowers in water you may as well throw them away," said Owen on the fourth day.

"I hope no one was expecting them," Janina said as she dropped them into the dustbin. But Owen had already gone.

The Earth continued its slow inevitable rotation. The clock ticked on. One of the cats meowed for more food. The exchange rate of the pound sterling fell in relation to the euro by one Polish złoty. The petals added droplets of colour to the potato peelings in the bin.

That night Janina had a dream that Gladys came back as a ghost. In the dream, Janina was trying to flush a very obstinate tampon down the toilet. Every time she pushed the button the tampon just got bigger and bobbed about in the water in an even less surreptitious way.

There was a queue of men outside the toilet. The men were getting very impatient and started banging noisily on the door. They were grey suited with ties and Janina felt sure they were from the City. She felt equally sure that if they came in and actually caught sight of the tampon, they would all become instantly ill. This would result in the pound becoming extremely unstable and the complete collapse of the Nikkei index.

It was a huge responsibility. How was she to save the whole of the twenty-first century capitalist economic system? And did she want to? She tried tearing a long strand of toilet paper off the roll and draping it over the tampon but it just pushed its way through, surfacing with apparent glee.

Just as the banging on the door got even louder, Gladys appeared. She was bigger than she'd been when she was alive. She had one leg missing and a look of revenge on her face. She promptly came to Janina's rescue by turning all the men into spiders, mating with them and then eating them. She paused only to ponder whether to mate with and then eat each one individually, or to mate with them one after the other and then end with a large banquet. It hadn't taken her long to decide on the latter.

Janina woke the following morning feeling decidedly happier; having a ghostly Gladys seemed an excellent idea and she started up her conversations with her again immediately. Miraculously, now that Gladys was a ghost, she could speak, or rather communicate, by sending telepathic messages. The trauma of dying a second time had obviously done the trick in restoring her grandmotherly memories.

That evening, after getting the girls off to bed, Janina managed a quick visit to the toilet for a chat with her invisible kinswoman. Her grandmother had never been keen on Owen in real life. She'd noticed that when he and Janina came to visit her on Sundays, Owen wiped his knife and fork on the tablecloth before eating, as if he thought she didn't clean her cutlery properly. As a result, she'd always made sure that he got the fatty bits of meat off the joint. Being drowned by him had done little to change her opinion.

"Letta zat bastard try anda getta me now," was Gladys' first telepathic contribution to the conversation.

4

As Janina was chatting to her seven-legged ancestor, Fatima
– proprietor of Fatima's Blossom Tree – was locking the
door of her shop and going upstairs to her flat. If Fatima's
customers were to imagine the proprietor of Fatima's Blossom Tree when the shop was closed (some being men, and
Fatima being an attractive woman, a number of them did)
they would conjure an image of her scantily clad as she
crafted bouquets for the following day, surrounded by lilies
and gladioli. But their vision was incorrect. By night, after
she'd cooked for her family and cleaned the flat, she parted
the leaves of books and arranged words instead of blooms.
Fatima's other passion was biography. Her speciality was
working on short memoirs of very ordinary people.

The rest of the family having gone to bed, nothing moved
in Fatima's flat except the cats, Salah and Violet, and
Fatima's pen. Because the stories were a record of people
otherwise unknown to the public, none of her readers
could be sure whether the chapters were biographies of real
personalities, whether they started off as real people but
Fatima transformed them into someone else, or whether
they were wholly fictitious. These written representations
had an unusual quality to them, something 'other', as if
their reality had been pressed – like petals – between the
pages of another world and turned into a vibrant print.
They were not strictly factual, yet they hinted at truth
through a tinted filter. She'd already decided that her next
piece of work would be about a woman named Lily, whom

she'd met recently. The opening chapter would begin:

Biography is a journey into the state of mistaken identity. It is a metaphor of life...

At the bottom of Janina and Fatima's back gardens, a massive urban park – gone to seed – sprawled for miles. It linked the inner-city streets to the outer housing estates. It was an otherworldly thoroughfare for cats to stroll, meet and cavort, weaving the destinies of their owners in the deepest shadows of ash and oak.

At the other side of the park were streets of neat semi-detached houses which, in the eighties, had been peopled by women who held Tupperware parties. Wineberry Drive was just one of those streets and, at number 114, lived Lily. While Fatima was writing and Janina was chatting to Gladys, a small but remarkable thing had happened at 114 Wineberry Drive.

Lily was at the other end of the room when it occurred. She heard a movement and turned to see the cat knocking an ornament off the mantelpiece. Lily hurried over but, by the time she got there, the ornament was already broken on the tiled hearth below.

"Well, that's that then," said Lily, as if she'd been waiting for this to happen.

If Lily had been asked to describe herself, she would probably have said she was Ernest's wife, even after Ernest was dead.

In her marriage she'd done everything for Ernest. She'd

given up her career for him. If Ernest was ill, she gave up her day out with friends for him. When he worried about her travelling alone, she gave up her holiday for his peace of mind. She cooked tapioca pudding (which if she'd taken the time to consider her own likes and dislikes, she would have discovered that she hated) every Tuesday evening for 40 years – all for Ernest. She'd had an unending repertoire of selfless acts through which she trudged mechanically.

If anyone had thought to ask her why she did it she'd have said it was for love. But no one did ask her and she wouldn't have thought to question these acts herself. They'd become a duty by unspoken agreement. Acts which maintain a balance of power are usually inconspicuous – only those that subvert it are visible. If love could be expressed in mathematical terms, Lily's love would have been a never-ending textbook of unequal mathematical equations of negations and sacrifices.

As part of her domestic duties, Lily had always done the dusting. Every day, she took the ornaments from the mantelpiece, wiped the wooden surface then dusted each ornament and put it back. They included two china figures of a shepherd and shepherdess. She and Ernest had bought them in the market years before when such figures had been popular. Lily had never been fond of them. Having them on the mantelpiece in the first place had been just one of many concessions she had made.

After Ernest retired, she noticed that one, or sometimes both, figures moved from the position she'd put them in the last time she dusted. The clock always remained in the same position, as did everything else, it was only the shepherd and shepherdess that shifted. She put them in one place and Ernest, without fail, placed them somewhere else.

The movement of the two china figures was like a dance. It started tentatively like the subconscious tapping of fingers, an expression of some hidden feeling. The expression was an inexact form of notation. It was trying to communicate something but was only able to do so in approximations. The couple danced with each other but their steps were not the same. They circled one another but were not a mirror image.

For Lily and Ernest, the time for shouting and arguing was over. Neither of them had been without passion, but Lily had capitulated over the years. The battleground of their domestic power struggles had shrunk to the rectangular area, 14 centimetres by 160, above the fireplace.

Neither Lily nor Ernest ever spoke about the dance. What Lily did know was that, on this matter, she wouldn't give in. It was a dance, or battle, for which there could never be a winner or a final step because no one knew the rules or the choreography. Even after Ernest died, the dance carried on. It was a process that Lily was unable to put an end to. She moved the ornaments for both herself and him, like a chess player with an imaginary opponent.

Ernest's death had been sudden. It was caused by the milk bottles. Although Lily had always done all the housework, Ernest put out the milk bottles. Decades earlier, when most milk rounds ceased to exist, the one in their area had continued. This allowed Ernest to persist with his one and only household chore. It was a task that he'd done with a glowing sense of self-sacrifice. He made such a song and dance about this daily performance that it took on the appearance of being the most time-consuming, and essential, act to be carried out in the list of household duties. Everything Lily had done in the last 24 hours paled to insignificance in comparison to this death-defying putting out of the milk bottles.

While Ernest was in hospital, and then at home in bed recovering from a mild heart attack, Lily hadn't put the milk bottles out. She'd come to believe over the years that only he could do it. Later she wondered why. Unless her husband somehow transported the milk bottles from the kitchen to the front door step with his penis, why couldn't she have done it? Later, she came to see that this had been a naive question because a professional footballer doesn't use his penis to play football (otherwise presumably the sport would have been given a very different name). Chairmen of multimillion-dollar corporations don't sign their multi-million-dollar agreements with their penises. And the top chefs of the world (we would hope) don't stir their soup with anything other than a kitchen utensil. Yet, on the whole, women remain a small minority in all these roles.

After a week recovering at home, Ernest managed to leave his bed and come downstairs.

"What are all those bloody milk bottles doing?" he demanded.

The row of bottles started halfway along the kitchen windowsill and overflowed, insolently, onto the kitchen table. He picked up an armful of them and staggered to the front door. The step was icy and he slipped, falling forwards. One of the milk bottles, still half in his arms, broke with the impact and a large splinter sliced straight through his jugular. It was a million-to-one-chance accident. It was so unlikely that Lily couldn't help wondering whether some ancient goddess had a hand in it. Ernest had portrayed putting out the milk bottles as a kind of ritual. Could the presence of the ritual have acted as a metaphysical doorway – a crack through which a feisty female deity could stretch an arm, just for a second, to give him his just deserts. A dessert which, in this instance, wasn't his favourite tapioca pudding.

He hadn't stood a chance. If the ambulance had got there quickly, he may have survived but the local health trust had recently privatised the area ambulance service (a move that Ernest had supported). The company that had won the bid had told their employers they would be paid a bonus if they kept their petrol costs down. As a result, towards the end of the week, the drivers kept running out of petrol. The ambulance crew who'd arrived at Lily's house had a social conscience. They always kept their tank well topped up. However, another unscrupulous crew had siphoned off their fuel while they were having a tea break.

The company was also not at all scrupulous about who it recruited and news soon got around. As a consequence, a number of the ambulance drivers were ageing former joyriders. They now had families to provide for and were attracted by the thought of being paid for careering, at speed, through traffic lights. However, they still automatically did a quick U-turn whenever they saw a police car. This made some patients feel more endangered by the ambulance ride than their illness. A number of poorly passengers decided their best chance of survival was to jump out of the back doors of the vehicle. Some of these unfortunate people hit their heads on the road as they landed. As a result, there was a gradually increasing population of vagrant amnesia sufferers in the area.

By the time the ambulance arrived for Ernest it was too late. His blood was mingling with the snow around the front door. The sticky, slightly congealed red substance on the surrounding white looked vaguely reminiscent of the strawberry jam that Ernest liked to put on his tapioca pudding.

5

When Owen told Dr Jelf that his wife didn't understand him, he'd actually been telling the truth. Janina would have admitted this. But Janina and Owen's view on this state of affairs was very different. Owen felt bitter, judgmental, towards Janina, whereas Janina would have expressed it as a plain fact of life. She had run out of energy with which to care.

Owen stood in front of Fatima's Blossom Tree. Fatima's cat twisted herself around his trousers.

"The capacity to care isn't infinite. The capacity to love isn't infinite. The capacity to hate even isn't infinite," he said to himself. "If none of these things are infinite, then what is?"

The cat started purring, blinking her delphinium eyes in pleasure, transcribing and retranscribing a figure of eight around his legs.

He was at a loss as to why his thoughts had taken such a philosophical turn on a Thursday afternoon. He made several attempts to go into the shop and each time he floundered in the doorway, between the lilies and the gladioli, and turned round again.

"The last time I got her flowers she didn't even put them in water," Owen confided in the cat. The cat paused a moment, arched her back, basking in his attention, then started on her figure of eight again, padding over the worn black and white floor tiles of the shop porch.

"Can I help?" Fatima came to the door delicately dusting yellow pollen from her T-shirt. The cat changed direction and elongated her figure of eight, binding it around her owner's legs as well as Owen's. She transcribed this larger figure twice then chose a smaller track between her owner's sandaled feet.

Owen told Fatima he was just looking and turned away. Then, because he had nothing better to do and was in need of a distraction, he decided to take his prescription from Dr Jelf to the chemist next door. Not that he was intending to take the tablets.

"One tablet to be taken as necessary," the pharmacist said. Owen took the bottle home and shoved it in the bathroom cabinet between a packet of ibuprofen tablets and some dusty face pack sachets that Janina had never got round to using. Then he left the house again. He'd decided to continue his philosophising over a pint.

Janina happened to be in the bar that Owen chose to have his solitary drink. There wasn't anything surprising about that, Wiley's bar was one of their locals.

Some of their locals were ones that Janina favoured and some were the ones that Owen preferred. They'd subconsciously apportioned the local eating and drinking establishments between them, giving each other space. It was similar to dividing shared belongings at the end of a relationship, except their relationship hadn't finished. Their marriage just went on under its own momentum as if it had forgotten why it existed in the first place and, therefore, didn't know how to bring itself to an end.

Owen heard Janina's voice as soon as he edged through the glass door. He recognised a couple of the people she was with. They were her interpreter friends. Janina had taught herself French at the age of eight, Hindi and Russian in her teens and studied Arabic and a variety of other languages at university. She'd become a translator and interpreter specialising in Eastern European, Arabic and South East Asian languages.

She was sitting with a pile of papers in front of her. Owen guessed they belonged to the manuscript she was translating. Her favourite kind of work involved mathematical, scientific and philosophical texts. Mathematics was another language that she spoke fluently. She'd studied for a second degree in Theoretical Physics and Pure Maths when the girls were small. The manuscripts she worked on ranged from the brand new, still steaming after being wrenched out of a contemporary scientist's cerebral cortex, to the ancient and obscure. She was often paid substantial amounts though, occasionally, she worked more for pure enjoyment – reclaiming previously lost insights from another time, another world.

She caught sight of Owen as he was making his way to the bar. She was putting her papers together into her backpack when he reached the table.

"Are you going?" asked Owen.

"Picking up the children," she said. There was no accusatory tone in her voice but Owen detected a subconscious glint of martyrdom in the angle at which she carried her bag.

He looked at his watch.

"Is it that time already?" he said. It wasn't the wisest of comments. He'd been late picking the girls up the week before.

"Perhaps I'll see you later," he called after her. He assessed the visibility of the fire exit signs and the clearance area around the emergency doorways. His comment hung in the air, self-consciously wondering whether it wanted to be taken sarcastically or not. By the time it had decided, Janina had already swung out through the door.

She drove the short distance to the school and sat in the car waiting. She itched to get the scientific text out of her bag. It was of ancient Arabic origin, expressing some startlingly different views on spatial relationships and putting forward the notion that larger structures could be nested within areas that were smaller than themselves. She knew that there wasn't enough time to look at it now so she gazed out of the car window at the empty playground instead.

If she strained her ears, she could almost hear the ghost-cries of children. Residual patterns from playtime games were engraved in the air above the bleak tarmac. Children's movements translated into energy lines captured in the atmosphere; geometric imprints of life, of passions. What area of curvature the height of joy? What obtuse angle the depths of despair?

6

After the demise of Ernest and of the shepherd, Lily started leading a more active life. A death dealt by the hand of an ancient goddess could have been an explanation for her sudden activity. But since Ernest's death, Lily had only half the amount of ironing to do. This mundane fact could have been the reason for her increased level of energy.

With the help of her sister, she'd made the funeral arrangements, and sang "Abide with Me" and "The Lord's My Shepherd". She dutifully read the cards and letters of condolence. She received deputations from the company Ernest had once worked for and bagged up most of his clothes to send to the charity shop. She explored with trepidation and guilt the strangeness of the left-hand side of the bed. She decided that when the house needed redecorating, she would do it in bright colours rather than the darker shades Ernest had decided, years ago, that they liked. She despatched a stockpile of tapioca pudding cans to the world's starving and she changed the milk order from two pints a day to just one pint every other day.

Three weeks after the ornament had landed on the hearth, Lily decided that what she needed was a holiday. It would help her get her life into perspective; a time to think, to let the old life recede into the past tense and the present to shape the future. She decided on a short holiday to the coast.

She sent her cat off to the cattery, with promises of extra treats on her return, packed a case and splashed out on a train ticket.

She didn't bother to book accommodation before she set off. There'd be plenty of bed and breakfast vacancies at this time of year. She wanted to look at them before she chose.

She felt a sense of excitement – almost a thrill – as she made her way from the station to the seafront. A number of the small boarding houses had 'no vacancy' signs. But when she reached the north bay, where gift shops and amusement arcades gave way to a disused boating pool and the occasional tea shop, she found a row of B&Bs all displaying vacancies. A large shaggy black cat with blue eyes jumped off the wall of one of the houses and wound itself around her legs. Then it walked in front of her as if leading her to a predetermined destination.

As soon as she saw the name Sea Witch Lily knew that this was where she wanted to stay. She was not put off by the fact that the front door wasn't painted quite as brightly as the others, the front garden was rather unkempt and the wooden fascia boards were peeling under the onslaught of salty sea spray. She smiled to herself as if she'd known that fate and her own feet would lead her to where she would be most comfortable. She stroked the cat's head and opened the front door.

Lily preferred the coast in winter and early spring when the beach and promenades were deserted. The influence of the moon on the Earth seemed like a tangible force, the battering of waves on land like a pagan rite as the gulls flew white, against a grey sky, above a grey sea.

The day after arriving, she walked along the front and watched the gulls. As a child, she used to turn her back on the taut string of the horizon and make believe that when she turned round again the gulls would have unravelled it, mixing the blue of the sky into the grey green of the sea.

Later she'd discovered that gulls cling onto air currents as limpets cling to the rocks below, although less heroically, for the limpets resist the pull of the tide while the gulls drift, with no resistance, on the moving eddies of air.

Lily had seen herself as a limpet but now she started to think she'd been like the gulls – inert, exerting no influence. She looked at her palms. She examined their lines as if they held an indecipherable message and made a decision.

She'd never had her fortune told. Her mother and father would have thought it wicked and Ernest would have thought it a wicked waste of money.

"Why shouldn't I do something wicked?" she said to herself. "As long as it doesn't harm anyone else."

She wasn't used to associating herself with wickedness. It felt youthful.

Clairvoyants' establishments were scattered at seemingly random or mystically assigned points along the promenade. Although Lily was later to find that their pattern was neither random nor ruled by divine intervention but regulated by the council. She looked at the names – Gypsy Rose, Anna Rosalie, Geraldine, Sarah (true descendent of the Great Laura Jane) – stopping when she reached Monica (granddaughter of the World Renowned Marlene). Monica herself was sitting in a green and white striped deck chair next to her doorway reading *Madame Bovary* and eating chocolate misshapes.

"I was expecting you, love," said Monica, turning down the corner of page 45.

"Were you?" Lily looked surprised.

"I felt it as I was eating my cornflakes this morning." Monica put another chocolate misshape in her mouth and offered one to Lily.

"I knew that a very attractive lady, not so young in years but young at heart, was coming to see me. That's right isn't it?"

Lily nodded and took a chocolate misshape, as if accepting it was part of a contract.

"In you come then and cross my palm with silver, although paper or plastic will do just as well."

Monica, not one to beat about the bush, pointed at the list of charges on the wall:

"Palm reading isn't it?"

Lily nodded again and handed over the money.

"You've had some unhappy times in your life. You've had a recent loss. Is that right, love? Is it the loss of someone close to you?"

She peered closely at Lily's hand.

"It's your husband. Good gracious me, killed by a milk bottle – an empty pint of full fat. I see a heart attack as well. Maybe he'd have been better off with semi-skimmed."

"That's what I kept telling Ernest, but he wasn't the sort of man to take advice."

Lily stopped. It was the first time she'd ever come anywhere close to criticising her husband to someone else. This was almost as surprising as hearing episodes of her life recited back to her as Monica gazed into her hand.

What she didn't know then was that the world-renowned Marlene Moule (grandmother of Monica) had recently been left some money in the will of a cousin. Marlene had decided to give up fortune telling and invest her bequest in a B&B, which she named Sea Witch. So, while Lily had tucked into her breakfast that morning, she had actually been enjoying a good chat with Monica's grandmother, while Houdini, Marlene's cat, had curled up uninvited on her lap.

The world-renowned Marlene Moule was having a cup of tea with her granddaughter when they'd seen Lily sauntering along looking with a mixture of interest and bewilderment at the fortune tellers' windows. They were trying a cup of freeze-dried granule tea to see if they could get a decent reading from the undissolved sediments. Marlene had quickly given Monica Lily's personal history before slipping off home through the back door.

"How about a cup of tea?" said Monica when she'd revealed, via Lily's palm, everything she could remember from the information passed on by her grandmother (and a little more besides from reading between the lines). Monica offered the cup of tea partly because she felt a genuine liking for Lily (for whom she'd promised a new and exciting life, teeming with unusual and intriguing people) and partly because it was a sales ploy she adopted when business was slack. Just as the customer was about to depart, Monica would notice something in the tea leaves and the customer would then cross her palm with the appropriate amount of silver for a reading.

Monica did see something very interesting in the teacup. She noticed that Lily had hidden psychic abilities, which Monica felt sure she should develop.

"That's odd, I see a woman talking to a dead spider called Gladys. I see a seven-foot bonsai tree with a cat and a parrot nesting in it and two crocodiles wearing nail varnish," said Monica as she swirled the cup round. Then she went quiet because she was seeing a forest growing in a house and an astral projection doing DIY. Monica presumed that these were faulty manifestations and decided that the sooner she gave up old-fashioned tea leaves and moved on to hi-tech granule readings, the better.

As she hurried back to supper at the Sea Witch, Lily thought about all she'd learned. She felt as if the afternoon had already begun heralding in the new life predicted for her.

"Monica said that she thought I had psychic abilities," she told Marlene, as she stirred the martini her landlady had given her.

"I used to have an interest in the occult and the psychic and that sort of thing myself," admitted Marlene Moule. "I'll let you have some of my old *Astro* magazines if you like."

Monica, Marlene and *Astro* magazine opened up a whole new world for Lily. She leafed through the pages with amazement. In places she'd had to withhold a growing urge to giggle, but it was still fascinating. There was advice for those who thought they'd been cursed. There were advertisements for runic divination, handwriting analysis, rituals and amulets, hypnotherapy, rebirthing and regression, chants and numerology. There was an advert for a deluxe book of spells that claimed it could cure a partner's snoring or a flea infestation, make your sexual fantasies come true, get rid of stubborn stains and decrease annoying condensation problems in the home.

It was a world Lily had been unaware of and it beckoned to her with an allure she found difficult to resist. She thanked Mrs Moule for the magazines and her enjoyable week and then caught the train home. She couldn't wait to find out more. Lily signed up for a year's subscription to *Astro* and enrolled on an online course in palmistry. She also wrote a stroppy letter to the milkman who'd left a note claiming long overdue arrears for bottles delivered some months ago. Then she bought some bright green paint for the living room.

"I feel," Lily said to her sister on the phone, "as if I've taken on a new astrological aura."

"That's very nice, I'm sure," said Lily's sister. "Just let me know if you want any help with the gardening."

7

While Lily was at the seaside, Janina had been confessing to Gladys that she was attracted to tall, intelligent men.

"Males of your species move around the world like existential removal men carrying the heavy furniture of ideology and placing it in inconvenient positions," said Gladys, who'd temporarily dropped the Italian accent and adopted one that sounded vaguely Liverpudlian.

Janina was surprised at Gladys' opinion, as well as her new method of delivery. Her grandmother had always held traditional views about gender roles. Her transformation into a spider had certainly radicalised her attitudes on women's issues.

Gladys informed Janina that her attraction to such men was a residue of women's culturally inherited desire to be dominated by men who were bigger and, by society's definition, stronger and more intelligent than them. This flaw had to be challenged. Gladys decided that Janina's hope of salvation lay in proving that she could be attracted to men who were short, weak and not very bright. She instructed Janina to take on a collection of lovers who fitted these criteria. It seemed odd advice for a grandmother to be dishing out but, with appropriate deference to her elders and not without qualms, Janina agreed, at least in part.

Although she and Owen had not had any dramatic arguments recently, their relationship had felt, like Owen himself, not quite real for some time. Janina thought the word to describe it might be *hovering*, like an indecisive swamp insect neither landing nor going anywhere but buzzing in an annoying way. She was too loyal to have an affair. Anything gained from an extra-marital relationship would be less than the feeling of discomfort that resulted from hurting Owen. But seeing if she could be attracted to a man displaying the attributes Gladys had stipulated – without instigating a physical or emotional relationship – might be an interesting experiment and, if conducted carefully, couldn't harm anyone.

Janina's first candidate was the deputy editor of a local paper. She knew him to be intellectually challenged, following a series of articles he'd recently written. As they'd never met, she wasn't sure whether his attributes fitted the other two essential criteria. It didn't take long to find out. Having spoken to him on the phone, she was soon sitting in the pub with him discussing a *Learn a Language for your Summer Holiday* column. First impressions were good. He turned out to be about five foot seven. He didn't look weak in an emaciated sense but there were no signs of muscles. If he had any, they were carefully concealed under a layer of flab. Surprised and flattered by her attention, he was only too pleased to meet up again the following week. This time their quasi-business discussion took place over dinner in a rather nice Italian restaurant, which had opened only a short while before.

It didn't go well. Conversation over starters was laboured. There'd been ideological differences of opinion while eating herb-scented cannelloni and she walked out on him in the middle of dessert. This was a shame, as it was a particularly good ice cream sundae. She never heard from him again and the holiday language-learning column was doomed before it had started.

Her second attempt was even less successful. This candidate was a small, hairy socio-biologist called Jasper from one of the local universities. She'd come across a review of his latest book in a journal. Janina didn't approve of much socio-biology, which in her view often used stereotypical concepts of human behaviour to incorrectly explain the actions of animals. In turn, this misinterpretation of animal behaviour was used to present current inequalities in human society as natural and unchangeable.

She met up with Jasper in the university refectory on the pretext of translating some of his work for the Eastern European market. Their next get-together, to firm up plans, was appropriately at the local zoo, followed by a meal in the same restaurant as the liaison with the deputy editor. Their relationship was already tricky by the time they passed the tiger enclosure and almost venomous by the time they reached the snakes.

When they arrived at the restaurant, she'd already had more than enough of him. She managed to smile and bite her lip through the starter (which was something of an achievement as it was minestrone soup). During the main course, Jasper put his hand on her leg while trying to put her right on a number of issues regarding apes. His hairy hand had started on her knee, then Janina felt the rough skin of his thumb run up the inside of her leg where it rested for a second while his chubby fingers gave her thigh a soft pinch. She removed his hand forcefully and rushed off to the toilet. She didn't return. She left the building, and his life, through a door next to the kitchen. Her only regret was the untouched ice cream sundae waiting for her on the table. She wondered what the socio-biologist would make of her actions and how he would use them to interpret the behaviour of some poor maligned meerkat or innocent giraffe.

The only close male friendship that she developed as a result of Gladys' instructions was with Bill Gupta. Bill was her third and final half-hearted attempt to save herself. She'd bumped into him, literally, while Bill was driving his car in the wrong direction round a roundabout. Why he'd been going round a roundabout in the opposite direction to everyone else is anyone's guess, but he'd collided with her car in the process. He'd not been drinking and Janina had the sneaking suspicion that he'd just been deep in thought. Bill had been a non-starter from the beginning. He didn't fit any of the necessary criteria because, although rather thin, he was just over six feet tall and possessed a higher than average intelligence.

She'd taken a liking to him almost immediately, and actually looked forward to meeting up with him to sort out her car repairs without involving insurance companies. They'd followed this first meeting with a meal at the same old restaurant. Janina was determined to actually eat an ice cream sundae. This time the conversation flowed, they had a natural rapport and, just before dessert, she confessed to Bill about her previous two visits to the restaurant and the reason behind them. Bill thought it was hilarious and they ended up having several coffees and a second ice cream sundae each. It was the start of a good friendship.

Janina ditched the erotic redemption plan the following day.

Her attempts at theoretical infidelity had proved useless in terms of achieving her original aims, though they'd had an unplanned side effect. In the way that early space missions had given us the non-stick frying pan, her own aborted mission had resulted in a more agreeable marriage. Compared to most of the new men in her life, Owen was certainly preferable. Janina was no nearer to landing on Jupiter's third moon, free from the gravitational pull of sexual hegemony, but domestic routine became easier. However, all non-stick frying pans start to build up a layer of burnt residue. Even the most advanced forms of Teflon do not retain resistant properties forever.

8

If having only half the amount of ironing to do since her husband's death explained Lily's dabbling in the occult, then having only half the amount of cooking and washing up might explain her growing involvement in subversive actions.

Lily's interest in benevolent activism, much like her immersion in the occult, occurred by accident. This time it happened when she discovered a book, *Projective Reactive Techniques: Soft Weapons Against the New Fundamentalism*, in the local library. Late spring had advanced into early summer and Lily enjoyed a long saunter through the park to the central library in the centre of the city. The book was in entirely the wrong section after an overworked, and momentarily distracted, librarian had got her Dewey classifications mentally tangled and misshelved it with books on mysticism. Lily was looking for a book recommended to her on levitation when she accidentally stumbled across it.

She took the book to a study bay and leafed through the pages. Despite herself she became absorbed.

The book suggested that twenty-first century fundamentalism was a cry for help. Fear, it claimed, was at the heart of all unbending creeds. It claimed there were no such things in society as oppressors or exploiters, only oppressed and exploited. Everyone, it said, was in some way exploited and oppressed.

"Even the traditional nineteenth century thinker, Marx, wouldn't have denied that the capitalist class are injured by their own economic system," the book stated on page three of the second chapter. "In some senses, the bourgeoisie lead just as spiritually limiting a life as the proletariat on whom their material wealth depends."

Lily leafed through the crisp pages distracted only by the occasional cough and the intermittent sound of heavy traffic seeping through the double-glazed windows.

"Should we not feel compassion for the billionaire CEO of a multi-national company almost as much as for the zero hours gig economy worker or the unemployed person on the corner of the street?" the book went on to ask.

She thought about the question. She took out a mint and sucked it hard. She felt that the writer's reasoning wasn't quite right. The man in the opposite study bay gave Lily a disapproving look as she crinkled the sweet paper. She raised one eyebrow and out-stared him, forgetting that she should be feeling sorry for his spiritually depleted life.

The book went on to talk about the uselessness of violence to subjugate oppression: "We must strive to understand those who subjugate others, encourage them to state their views and in so doing start the process of healing," Lily read out loud to herself. "Show them some compassion, draw them into conversation to find out why they feel the need to oppress."

She decided to borrow the book along with *Colour Therapy and the Study of Chakras* and a cookery book entitled *Cooking as a Symbolic Art Form*. She read the books avidly. She'd always enjoyed reading as a girl. When she was young, she'd had a subterranean non-conformist streak. As a child, she'd pronounced herself to be a conscientious objector, should there be a Third World War, and her parents had called in the vicar to talk some sense into her. Later on, she'd sold Trotskyite papers in pubs, although she hadn't fully understood what Trotskyism was. She met her future husband soon after that and never owned up to either of these stains on the tablecloth of her past life. Instead, she carefully covered the blemishes with the condiments and cutlery of domesticity. Now Lily had cleared the table and revealed the spills from her previously brimming life. She'd allowed life to pass her by for a while, and now she wanted to catch up – to soak in everything she'd been oblivious to during her marriage. The process of absorption was both exhilarating and painful, like blood rushing back into numbed limbs.

She changed physically. She was larger, as if her body was unfolding, increasing its surface area to absorb more of the world around her. As life soaked through her receptive skin, she solidified. An osmosis was taking place. A partial invisibility, which had characterised Lily in her adult life, was disappearing itself – revealing the woman beneath.

Another reason for her greater visibility was her increased appetite. The cookery book had fired her culinary imagination. Now, she saw food as something that could satisfy her own tastes and wishes rather than Ernest's. Meal times became new sensory experiences. As Lily sat in front of the television with a large plate of couscous and Moroccan spiced meat and vegetables, she imagined what Ernest's reaction would have been. She conjured up from her memory a vision of her late husband. He now had a large scar on his neck.

"What's that disgusting stuff?" he asked. Death had done nothing to make him more congenial.

"A tagine and it's delicious," she said out loud, holding up a piece of dripping lamb on her fork. "It's North African."

The scar on Ernest's neck pulsed before he pixelated into the wallpaper.

Lily started to mix up a heady and potent three-course meal of philosophies. She took her ingredients and she peeled, chopped, stirred, marinated, braised and garnished them to produce her own realisation. She fused the absorbed concepts with the flavour of her experiences. She was a politico-culinary device waiting to go off in a herb-infused explosion of new ideas. In her mind, notions on dialectics simmered with theories of invisibility. She carried out her own unconventional research programme using astral charts to explain the success or failure of different historical events. She was giving birth to her own individual philosophy. It wrenched her insides as it struggled towards life, whooping a yell of triumph as it took its first hungry breaths of air.

Her new philosophy was one that craved action. Her first action was to liberate the life forms interred by her husband in the garden and the greenhouse. She thought it wrong to wilfully stunt the natural growth of a living organism so she released the bonsai trees. She took them out of the greenhouse and put them on a bodybuilding diet of fortified plant nutrients. When she had time, she read them extracts from Simone de Beauvoir or played them downloads of Edith Piaf.

She took out the strips that divided the lawn from the flowerbeds and allowed the grass to advance into the soil. She introduced creeping thyme to the cracks between the paving stones so when she stepped on them on the way to the washing line they released a woody aroma. Nature helped. A wild rose sucker latched onto one of her husband's favourite bushes and irises spread to where Ernest had never intended irises to be. Sage invaded the lawn.

Frogs appeared from nowhere, hopping amongst the

roots of honesty plants that had grown from seeds blown into the garden from who knows where. Lily introduced forget-me-nots, eucalyptus and fig. She planted honeysuckle, Peruvian lilies, sea lavender, a flowering peach, an almond tree. She seeded rosemary, tamarix, witch hazel, apricot, barberry, artichoke, acacia and quince. A lush-foliaged, heavy-scented green and crimson abundance stealthily invaded the garden.

While voluptuous disorder took hold of the garden by hard work and design, an unpremeditated anarchy took a toehold in the house through pure neglect. Spiders spun webs across the living room ceiling and a caterpillar metamorphosed undisturbed into a chrysalis on the dining room windowsill. The cats alternately languished luxuriantly on the powder blue candlewick bedspreads and rolled and cavorted on the scented lawn.

"There's something more therapeutic about toiling in the garden than fighting to maintain a status quo indoors," Lily told her cat and a flowering cactus.

Lily felt purposeful. She felt fit. She felt mentally enriched and stimulated. After a while Lily thought how nice it would be to share her new found enthusiasms with other people. She'd taken advantage of a number of online courses on various subjects of interest, but the virtual discussions were not as satisfying as face to face interactions. She decided to enrol on a part-time college course.

"You've left it a bit late," the woman in the office said when Lily went to the local adult education centre. "All the classes are full apart from *Later 20th Century and Early 21st Century Politics.*"

"That sounds perfect," said Lily.

9

It took Janina a week to read the Arabic text on inverse spatial relationships. It had been interesting but frustrating. Janina told Gladys all about it on Sunday evening. The invisible spider had moved from her cramped lodgings in the downstairs toilet to an invisible web in the upstairs bathroom.

"Its value is in its uniqueness but because of its uniqueness some of what it says is totally incomprehensible," said Janina. "There are parts that I can't translate. Without understanding the wider concepts, I can't comprehend the individual words and, without being able to decipher the words, I can't grasp the larger concept."

"Mamma mia," said Gladys, who was back in Italian mode. "Whata can you do?"

"The writer's meaning is in there in the structure but I can't get to the centre of it. It's like a labyrinth," said Janina.

After due consideration, Gladys suggested that if she couldn't find direction from within the book then perhaps she should look elsewhere.

Janina took her advice and studied another manuscript of Polish origin that was more modern and discussed the relationship between idealism and materialism. Then she stood in the bedroom looking in the wardrobe. Doing so made her wish even more that she could translate the old Arabic text.

From being a small child, Janina had always wanted her own wardrobe. It was one of the big ambitions in her life.

She was aware that some people would regard this as a flippant ambition when they themselves had more challenging aspirations, such as being the chief executive of Microsoft, or more righteous wishes like saving the rainforests or ridding the world of hunger and disease. But Janina was sure they all had a wardrobe of their own. If not, this seemingly self-centred desire would have replaced all their more altruistic goals.

When she was small, Janina had been expected to use a section of her parent's wardrobe. She'd progressed onto sharing with her sister. When she was a student, she'd had no wardrobe at all and simply folded her clothes and put them in a small cupboard or draped them over chairs. Finally, she shared a wardrobe with Owen.

If Janina could have understood the Arabic text, she could have solved her own and the world's storage problems, taking some pressure off the dwindling rainforests at the same time. But she didn't. And now she had a more immediate problem –she couldn't find her favourite blue dress.

The innards of the wardrobe were a disturbing sight – a snapshot of an inanimate skirmish. Had she looked at the same contents a few years earlier she would have seen it differently. At the beginning of her relationship with Owen, there'd been something positive about sharing because Janina had assumed she and Owen were sharing equally. The arms of Owen's shirt had draped affectionately over the shoulder of her turtleneck jumper. His jacket leant sensually against her lilac blouse. Their trouser legs knotted around each other passionately. Later, she'd realised that not only had Owen failed to do any cooking for three months but he'd also got more than sixty-five per cent of the hanging space in the wardrobe. The affectionate drape of the shirt looked more like a restraining arm, and the legs of his work trousers a half-hearted rugby tackle.

When Janina finally found her dress, it was rolled up on the floor of the wardrobe. It was badly creased and had a small rip in it. A pair of Owen's muddy climbing boots sat proudly on top of it.

It was too much. She tried to eat her Sunday roast as if everything was normal but it wasn't possible. She left in the middle, giving her reasons but, at this stage, not stating the terms and conditions of her return – if, in fact, there was to be a return. She took a couple of ibuprofen, knocking over Owen's bottle of tablets and spilling the contents into the cabinet in the process. She grabbed the face packs on a whim. She might actually have time to use them while she was away. Perhaps exfoliation would help her emerge with a new skin into a fresh life. She decided to leave Lidka and Eve with Owen. It would do him good to take responsibility and the girls would benefit from seeing more of their father. She would miss them terribly but to drag them off to cramped, makeshift lodgings in a friend's house would not be beneficial for them. It would be better to let them stay put in the comfort of their own home with their own belongings and their own friends. She reminded them to feed the cats, Gus and Carlotta, as Owen, no doubt, would forget all about them.

She phoned Bill Gupta.

"Your timing is perfect," said Bill, before Janina could ask if she could be a house guest for a few days. "Come right over, I need help."

10

Bill rented the second floor of a house in which his land-lady occupied the ground floor. When Janina arrived, he was looking pale and had a wild look in his eyes. His finger was bleeding profusely.

"I'm going away for a week," Bill's landlady had said to Bill one day as they passed in the hallway. "You don't mind feeding Myrta, my cat, for a few days, do you?"

Bill did mind.

"Of course not," he said. It was hard to refuse because the conversation was taking place in the hallway. It gave the subject a feeling of marginal importance, as if it wasn't a very big favour and that refusing would be churlish. Had his landlady knocked on his door and a longer conversation taken place, it would have given the subject more gravity and made it easier to refuse. Once the words *of course not* had slipped out, Bill knew it was a big mistake. His feelings towards cats wasn't just dislike, it was an irrational fear. But how could he say it was an impossibility now he'd agreed? A longer sentence would have been easier to overturn but the three words he'd uttered, like the area of the house in which he'd uttered them, were flimsy. They were too light to get a good grip on – they had already floated away.

Bill practised excuses in his bathroom mirror.

"My mother is ill and I must visit her in the hospital," he said. It sounded like a sentence waiting for translation in an Open University modern languages programme.

Similarly, "I need to travel to a conference in Helsinki,"

was obviously from an online Finnish course.

Because his mind had turned to the notion of language lessons, he could only think of obscure sentences that might be found in old-fashioned French text books.

"I must help my aunt refill her fountain pen. I must assist my grandfather in waxing his moustache. My brother needs my aid in repairing his punctured bicycle wheel."

While his mind was grabbing for possibilities, his land-lady knocked on his door.

She had the key to her kitchen in her hand and looked as if she knew what Bill had been up to.

"There's a cat flap so you don't need to let her in and out. Just feed her twice a day. She doesn't need anything till breakfast tomorrow morning," she said.

Before Bill could protest, she'd retreated down the stairs.

Breakfast went without mishap. He'd got up early and gone down to the kitchen before he did anything else. He'd managed to put the cat's food in the bowl while she was out. He could see her through the kitchen window, her tail twitching while she watched an unsuspecting sparrow on the lawn. Bill shivered just looking at her. He went back upstairs, showered, dressed, had breakfast and went out. He was gone for a long time. Perhaps it was unavoidable or perhaps he was purposely delaying his return knowing that he would have to go through the feeding routine again.

Myrta was lying in wait for him as he opened the front door. She meowed enthusiastically. Throat tightening, Bill edged his way down the hallway.

He took the key out of his pocket and unlocked the kitchen door. He took the can of cat food from the cupboard, trying to ignore the insistent warmth of the feline body winding round his legs. His fingers trembled as he yanked the ring pull. Fear had pumped adrenaline into his hands, resulting in too much strength and physical tension in his fingertips. The ring pull snapped off. By this stage, Myrta was rubbing her body expectantly between his ankles, meowing insistently. Bill tried to open the cat food with a can opener. He was all thumbs. The longer he took the more the cat meowed, and the more the cat meowed the more hopeless his attempts to open the can became. He picked up a knife. An accident was inevitable. He tried to staunch the blood under the kitchen tap while Myrta wailed and fixed him with her blue moon eyes.

Janina staunched the blood and then decided Bill needed time to recuperate on his own. She'd have to stay elsewhere. Promising to come back to help with his cat sitting duties the following day, she decided to swallow her pride and make friends with Celia Jelf.

The journey took a while even though Janina drove slightly above the speed limit once she was out of the urban area. Celia lived in the countryside. The area was low lying and often flooded. It felt far from civilisation. The car had to be left half a mile away from the cottage, and the rest of the way walked.

The path meandered over the vestiges of an old moor. The ground was spongy underfoot, giving slightly as she walked. It was an eerie feeling, as if she'd entered a three-dimensional watercolour. The air was saturated, the land-scape floating precariously on a thin film of oil. Greens, yellows and ochres held their forms of grass, trunk and shrub, ready at any moment to run into each other to become only raw substance, reverting into unpremeditated pattern.

Janina knocked on the cottage door, wondering whether she would be welcome.

"I thought you'd taken your germs elsewhere," said Dr Jelf.

"I have. I've left my malevolent micro-organisms at home," said Janina.

"Let me guess," said Dr Jelf. "You've left that husband of yours. The man who doesn't exist."

"I'm not interrupting anything am I?" asked Janina.

"Only my solitary wading in depression," said Dr Jelf. "Shall we crack open a bottle of brandy?"

"It's bad for your health," said Janina.

"Being a GP's bad for your health," said Celia Jelf. "But I still do it."

Janina collapsed onto Dr Jelf's large comfortable sofa and eased off her muddy shoes.

"It's male hierarchies," said Janina, after a couple of brandies. "You should be at the top of your profession by now."

"But do I really want to be at the top of a hierarchy?"

"When you think about it," said Janina. "Hierarchies are phallic symbols so it goes without saying that the higher you climb the more of a dick you become."

"Well, that's my future sorted out then," said Dr Jelf. "I'll stay in the gentle clitoral foothills. Now, what about your problems?"

On Monday morning, Janina cancelled a couple of meetings. She sat and read Celia Jelf's magazines. The surgery's health visitors read magazines voraciously and donated them to the waiting room once they'd finished with them. Janina, knowing where Celia shamelessly pilfered them from, read them at arm's length so as not to catch anything unpleasant. There were articles on next winter's high street fashion predictions, belly dancing, how to look after parrots and recycling old clothes. She relieved the monotony by helping Bill with Myrta.

"Did everything go alright?" Bill's landlady asked on her return.

"No problem," said Bill. But he'd decided that he'd move, in case his landlady ever asked the same favour again. He was going to stay at a friend's flat for a week. When the friend returned, he was to share a house with his sister, Gertie. He'd already started packing some of his belongings. He'd also told his pet hamster.

After three days Owen phoned Janina.

"I know you think you'd be better off without me," he said. "What is it you want to do in your new life?"

The question took Janina by surprise. For a moment she couldn't think of what to say. Then she thought of the magazines she'd been reading.

"For a start," she said. "I'll buy a parrot and go belly dancing."

II

Václav Havel arrived on Lily's lap just as she finished reading a book on the Cuban Revolution and was deciding which to read next, *Bin Laden: Twenty-First Century Fundamentalism* or *The Orange Struggles of the Ukraine Revisited*. He appeared through the window and landed, with a thump, on top of a photo of the late Osama Bin Laden, spilling tea out of the cup Lily had just been replacing on its saucer.

"Good gracious. Where did you appear from?" asked Lily. Then she noticed the pendant hanging from the cat's collar. It bore his name but no telephone number or address.

She realised that either this was the late Václav Havel, the playwright who'd been the president of the Czech Republic until 2003 and was said to have died in 2011 but had instead, perhaps, metamorphosed – Kafka-style – into a large domestic cat, or a lost cat with an unusual name. If the first scenario was correct, she thought she might know where to return him. She'd learned in her evening class that President Havel had lived in the top floor flat of a house on Rasinova Nabreszi on the Right Bank of the Nové Město area of Prague.

He was now staring knowingly at her from a higher vantage point after climbing to the top of one of the bonsai trees, which had now grown to a height of seven feet.

That evening, Lily stood in her garden shouting: "Václav, Václav!"; feeling as if she was in a twentieth century demonstration in Wenceslas Square rather than calling a cat in for his supper.

Václav was actually already safely back in the living room. He'd sneaked through Lily's legs and into the kitchen while she'd been calling his name. He was getting acquainted with Lily's own cat, a tortoiseshell called Frida Kahlo (as a result of the dark smudges of black fur above her eyes). Václav and Frida sat quite companionably watching the news and looking at each other out of the corner of their eyes. Lily came back into the room just too late to hear how the Nikkei, the FTSE and the Dow Jones were all doing peculiar things and that the next programme was to be a wildlife documentary on the mating habits of the spider.

"Oh, there you are President Havel," she said. "How about some Whiskas?"

It was when the repair man refused to come back with a new part for her malfunctioning tumble dryer in case he got bitten by some species of animal previously thought to be extinct (except in the swampier regions of the Venezuelan rainforest) that Lily had to accept that strange things were happening in her home.

Some analysts of Czech literature hold the view that the distinctive internal architecture of Prague's older buildings directly influenced the content of Kafka's writing. With Lily's home, an inverse relationship had developed. Her feverish writing had brought about concrete changes to the architecture of her house.

One day, Lily got out the vacuum cleaner and realised that her gardening tools would now be more appropriate. She tried to look at her home through the eyes of a stranger. What she saw was rather exciting. The more she examined her home, the more peculiar it became, as if scrutinising it caused further metamorphoses.

It was a while since she'd ventured into her dining room because she'd taken to eating her meals on a tray in front of the television. She opened the door and stepped in. The cats followed. Frida Kahlo took three steps sideways, her back arched, and Václav Havel tried to look unconcerned, but the fur on his neck stood up in little points.

The houseplants had flourished so that they appeared to belong to totally different species to the ones they'd originally been associated with. Creepers crawled up the walls and over the ceiling, creating a green canopy and bestowing the room with a murky green twilight. The faint but unmistakable call of birds and animals came from the undergrowth that concealed the wall and window. Lily pushed her way through, stretching her hands out in front of her, reaching for the anticipated dining room wall. She took one, two, three steps and more. It appeared the dimensions of her house had altered – extended. The undergrowth gradually gave way, not to the solidity of brick covered by plaster but to an open grassy area. It was bounded on the far side by trees that looked as if they were the edges of a forest.

Lily was wondering how safe it would be to explore the forest when she heard her front doorbell ring. For a moment she was tempted not to bother answering but the sound had such urgency that Lily felt she must.

The woman on the doorstep was the florist who'd done the flowers for Ernest's funeral. She and Lily had got on surprisingly well, especially under the sober circumstances. They'd got into conversation about storytelling and Lily had told the florist that she'd be most welcome to call by some time.

Fatima was bearing a bouquet of flowers. Lily invited her in.

12

Lily showed Fatima into the living room. A quick glance at her footwear convinced Lily that this was a more suitable venue than the dining room. The florist was wearing sling-back sandals, not the sort of shoes for afternoon tea in a forest clearing, which Lily guessed might be quite soggy underfoot. Besides, Lily wasn't sure what reaction Fatima would have. She was aware that some people might view having a forest in one's dining room as an indicator of poor standards of housekeeping.

Lily tucked a few stray *Astro* magazines under the sofa and dusted off her best china teacups.

"I thought I'd pop round and see how you were coping," said Fatima.

"To be honest," said Lily. "I've never been better."

"Well, everyone deals with loss in different ways," said Fatima, glancing around the dusty room. Václav Havel was perched at the top of his favourite bonsai tree. He looked very much like one of her neighbour's cats that had disappeared some weeks before.

Lily watched Fatima's face carefully, and as she didn't detect any judgement, she decided to be frank.

"It's sometimes difficult to see it as a loss," said Lily. "A loss to Ernest of course, but not a loss to me. I've come to realise that poor Ernest was an old misery."

She put her cup on her saucer and smiled reassuringly at Fatima: "He cooked his own goose in the end. It's the only thing he did cook in the whole forty-odd years I was married to him."

Fatima laughed loudly. Then covered her mouth.

"Oh, I'm so sorry," she said.

"Why be sorry? Laughing's good for you," said Lily. As her new friend was still looking unnecessarily contrite, she decided to change the subject. "How are you getting on with your biographies?"

"I finished writing my grandmother's story a few weeks ago," said Fatima. "But it was very sad. She was married off at the age of sixteen to a madman. She had a baby but couldn't stop weeping. She believed that if she lived forever, she'd still not have time to cry for everything in the world that deserved a tear."

"It's criminal," said Lily, "that any woman's definition of the infinite should be measured in unstoppable tears. What happened to her?"

"She died when the baby was still small," said Fatima. "Her husband gave the baby to his sister. The child grew up wanting for nothing – except for the knowledge of his mother."

Both Lily and Fatima took another biscuit as a belated affirmation of Fatima's grandmother's life – an unspoken, all-butter, pleasingly crunchy act of solidarity.

"I think maybe she was suffering from postnatal depression," said Fatima. "I think I had it too, when I had my second child. While I was still in hospital my identity bracelet came off and I believed the hospital staff had paired me with the wrong baby."

She paused to see how Lily was taking this. As she was calmly choosing another chocolate digestive from the packet on the table, Fatima continued.

"Because they'd paired me off with the wrong baby, it was a natural consequence that I was sent home to the wrong family."

"A natural escalation of the error once they'd made the first mistake," said Lily, indistinctly because her mouth was full of biscuit. "If people were a little more aware, they'd know that life's full of peculiar little accidents like that. Did your family comment on any difference in you?"

"Not that I recall," said Fatima. There was a pause in the conversation for a few moments while both women contemplated whether to have another digestive.

"Postnatal depression might explain why you thought you'd been sent home with the wrong baby to the wrong family," said Lily. "It doesn't explain why your family didn't notice they'd been sent home the wrong woman."

"My life has often felt as if it's all disconnected parts," said Fatima. "Now, I want to stand back and look at my whole life."

Lily thought of Fatima as a sign painter on a ladder who, after spending a long time copiously painting a series of letters, has the urge to step back and see what they spell.

Fatima was about to step back.

13

After spending a few days at Celia Jelf's, Janina had to go on a trip to Poland. It had been planned some time before. She'd already agreed with her mother, Zosia, that her daughters, Lidka and Eve, would stay with her while she was away. Owen was going to be out of town as well on a climbing expedition in France. There'd been an argument about it, as Owen had forgotten to mention it to Janina. He hadn't realised, until almost the last minute, that it clashed with Janina's commitment. Janina had sorted the potential disaster out by asking her neighbour to feed the cats, Gus and Carlotta, and by asking her parents if the girls could stay with them.

"It's no big deal," Owen had said. "Your parents love to have the girls."

This was true. Zosia and Robert were delighted to have Lidka and Eve but it irritated Janina that Owen could be so cavalier about the whole thing. It was especially annoying because her journey was work related while his was simply a climbing excursion. This argument had lost its rancour with the more recent drama over the crumpled dress and the fight over wardrobe space.

Janina picked the girls up from home on the day she was to fly to Warsaw. She limited her communications with Owen to an uncomfortable minimum and drove quickly over to her mother's house. Janina hadn't told her parents about her argument with Owen.

"I told you that you could never trust a man who wears slip-on shoes," said Zosia, after the girls promptly and delightedly revealed the details of their parents' falling out.

"Owen wears lace-ups most of the time. He can hardly go climbing in slip-on boots. And anyway, Dad wears slip-on shoes for gardening," said Janina, pointing through the patio doors to her father digging in the vegetable patch.

Zosia looked at her husband and then back at her daughter with a meaningful twist of the eyebrows. Janina was glad the girls were there. She could think of only one thing worse than talking to her mother about her own relationship problems.

"Anyway," said Zosia, "make sure you get half of everything."

"I'm not sure it's going to come to that," said Janina.

At the bottom of the garden, Robert was wiping the sweat from his forehead with his sleeve, taking a break for a moment while the next-door neighbour chatted to a visitor. Janina could almost see her father's ears waggling as he listened. Robert collected information. Not newsworthy or useful information, but verbal trivia. He took a pride in finding out as much about other people as possible without divulging any information about himself.

"Just look at him earwigging," said Zosia, standing beside Janina. "Yet he gets cross if I tell anyone anything. You'd think I'd committed some capital crime if I tell the neighbours anything we're doing."

Janina knew this was true. Her father seemed to believe that each gram of information given away diminished you – in the same way that some cultures believed that having your photograph taken eroded your soul. She'd sometimes seen her father standing in the kitchen doorway while her mother chatted to the neighbours. He'd wave his arms impatiently muttering her name in an infuriated way under his breath, as if she were about to reveal state secrets to a hostile nation.

"I always buy butter. I don't like vegetable spread," Zosia might say quite innocently to the woman next door. But in Robert's eyes, a piece of his soul weighing approximately four grams bit the dust. Ten more statements like that and a whole arm's worth of soul would be needlessly discarded. Where did her father think these pieces went? Perhaps they evaporated into the air, transposed like moisture into the water cycle. Later, Robert would try and redress the balance. A poacher of souls creeping along the alley at the back of the urban gardens, he would listen for shouted titbits or cajole facts from careless neighbours.

He kept a diary as his confidante. Into its pages, he scribbled each evening all the facts he guarded so closely in daylight. Between the ruled lines, he spilled details of how much tax he'd paid that year, the cost of his new shirt, the interest he was paying on a loan – the unspeakable figures of his existence. They were detached from emotions and actions. A dangerous catalogue kept in a locked drawer.

"Mashed or boiled?" Zosia asked her daughter, bored with watching her husband eavesdropping.

"Mashed would be nice," said Janina, following her mother into the kitchen to lend a hand with peeling.

Zosia kept a diary as well but her pages were filled with a mix of related to-ings and fro-ings of the day and her nightly dreams. She never missed a day. If at a later date some statement or accomplice was required, everything would be carefully in place. She took it for granted that the happenings in her dreams would be just as important as those of her waking hours. Zosia's other main pastime was her sewing, mainly embroidery. Her tastefully stitched pictures hung on the wall. While Robert grew his flowers and trees in the garden, she preferred to grow her flowers and trees from thread.

Her parents had always seemed ill-matched to Janina, as if they'd been thrown together by some miscalculation and that both would have been happier if they'd married someone else. She'd never given a thought to how the girls viewed her relationship with Owen. As they got older, it was inevitable that they'd make their own appraisals. She looked at Lidka and Eve playing bagatelle in the living room, then started to cut crosses in the base of each of the sprouts her mother handed her.

Janina would have been happy with a salad. It was Zosia who'd insisted on cooking a Sunday roast. Zosia had become a competent, though fairly plain cook in response to Robert's traditional English tastes. A few slices of grilled kaszanka alongside the roast chicken and a dish of Polish gherkins to accompany the meal were the only hints of cultural diversity.

After the meal, Janina had a cup of tea, ate a slice of her mother's Victoria sponge cake, hugged and kissed the girls goodbye and left her parents doing the dishes. Her mother was washing, her father drying. It was an unwritten agreement cast many years ago. Perhaps they were happy with each other despite the messages her mother often tried to convey with her eyebrows.

14

Janina always slept with her eyes open. It was a trait she'd inherited from her great-grandmother. Some people found this characteristic unnerving and those who didn't know about it often took Janina to be awake when she was sleeping. This was why the steward on the flight to Warsaw asked if Janina would like a drink, waking her in the process, rather than leaving her peacefully to her dreams.

The plane started to descend, taking wide circles while it queued. Looking through the window, it seemed to Janina that the summer heat had curled around the whole continent. The cities of Europe were panting in the sun. High-rise blocks were wilting in the shimmering haze. Shopping centres, like giant lizards with their feet caught in melting tarmac, could only dream of darting beneath cool rocks. Their stone skin sizzled in the heat. Old men in small town bus stations all over Eastern Europe would be sitting on benches, picking out and eating the seeds from sunflower heads, spitting the shells into the dry dust around their feet.

After a few minutes, the plane landed in the sweating city. Janina got a cab through the airless streets to her hotel. She hadn't stayed in it before. It was an older building, newly refurbished, and she was pleased to find that she had a top floor room with a good view of the urban sprawl. She unzipped her weekend bag and hung her clothes with a luxuriant flourish in the gaping space of the huge wardrobe.

Then she went out into the heat. She sat down to read on a bench beneath a tree but found it hard to settle. Feeling dehydrated, she made her way back to the hotel and, after a quick room service snack and a bath, she went to bed. She had a meeting at ten thirty the following morning. It took Janina a while to drop off.

Originally, she'd been coming to Warsaw to meet two clients but one had cancelled. She'd been unsure whether one client was enough justification for coming all the way to Poland. The meeting could, quite adequately, be tackled by video call. A feeling of guilt compounded this uncertainty. She could have cancelled the meeting when she'd found out about Owen's plans. But, in some ways, Janina had welcomed the problem – basking in the possibility of an affray with Owen.

Then she'd received an email from someone she had known well a long time ago. He was going to be in Poland at the same time. She'd agreed to meet up. It gave more purpose to the journey – a convenient added justification for going. It was this social appointment that was keeping Janina awake.

15

When Fatima arrived home from Lily's house, she was pleased to discover that she didn't need to cook. The cat had already produced the evening meal. Fatima presumed it was the cat as she couldn't imagine that anyone else in the household would have had the presence of mind to do it.

Fatima had stayed at Lily's for three hours, which is why the cat had seized the opportunity to showcase her culinary skills. The casserole – of adventurously varied ingredients – gave off an unusual aroma. It had a fishy smell that reminded Fatima, suspiciously, of the new cod roe-in-jelly cat food she'd recently bought Violet as a treat. But which Violet, with predictable feline pernicketiness, had refused to eat.

Violet was the first-generation offspring of a kitten Fatima brought back when she'd visited her cousin in Morocco – the country from which their family originated.

The square in the town where her cousin lived was over-run with emaciated wild cats. Fatima had plucked an almost-grown black tom kitten with eyes as lavender-blue as jacaranda petals from the dust. She'd put him through quarantine and adopted him. Salah, her husband, thought she was crazy. She named the kitten after him to annoy him even more.

"You great hairy layabout, Salah," Fatima shouted now and then, turfing him off the sofa where he was lolling next to his human namesake. The double meaning wasn't lost on either husband or cat.

Meggie, next door's little tabby, was rather tubby but she

wasn't without feminine wiles. She and Salah enjoyed a noisy whirlwind romance under a crescent moon. Violet was their love child (or, at least, one of them). Salah's wanderings, and his romancing of the local she-cats, had spawned blue-eyed kittens all over the neighbourhood, weaving a feline kinship network with unseen veins of attachment coursing through the underbelly of the urban sprawl. Salah disappeared for days on end but Violet was a stay-at-home cat, never venturing much further than next door to visit her mother, sisters and brothers. After her unaccustomed culinary efforts, she was sleepy and purred loudly. Fatima stroked her. She appreciated her help, especially as Salah had, unashamedly, tried to take the credit – pretending he knew where the pans were kept and how to turn on the oven.

During their visit, Fatima and Lily had quickly built up a rapport. It confirmed to Fatima that the older woman would be wonderful inspiration for a story. She emanated a vibrancy that was energising. At the same time, Fatima's receptiveness to her ideas was just what Lily needed. At last she'd found someone with whom she could discuss her new philosophies.

Lily lent Fatima three books so, after the rest of her family had gone to bed, Fatima brewed a pot of tea and curled up on the sofa with them. She read them out loud to herself and the cat. Violet, still worn out from her culinary endeavours, kept dropping off, waking then dozing off again and, as a result, developed a rather unique understanding of post-Marxist-feminism and a skewed concept of the links between ideology and collective action. Had Violet known any cats with a grasp of classical Marxism, and had she discussed her own views with them, they'd probably have called her a revisionist pig. But she didn't, so it didn't matter.

It was a humid night and when Fatima went to bed she found it difficult to sleep. It was partly the stimulating conversation with Lily, partly the content of the books, partly Salah snoring beside her and partly the cat's cooking. There was the occasional sound of a siren and, if it was close enough, the squealing of brakes as an ambulance from the privatised service that had sealed the fate of her new friend's husband U-turned to avoid a police car. The vehicles were usually too far away for Fatima to hear the banging door as a traumatised patient jumped out, potentially bumping their head and joining the city's small but swelling band of amnesiacs.

She tossed and turned under sweaty sheets in an area between sleep and wakefulness. She was thinking about something her cousin had once told her. Ancient Egyptians, she'd said, believed that cats are pre-emptive shadows – the paths they walked silently wove together the lives of humans. It was a piece of information that had appeared in Fatima's life unexpectedly upsetting the teacup of everyday appearances.

When she eventually dropped off, she dreamt of waking in a strange place to the sound of running footsteps and a man shouting. The shouting sounded desperate, crazed like a madman, and the direction of the footsteps appeared confused, like a person unable to find their way out of a maze. The noises came from behind a door, so she opened it, just a crack, to peep through. She had no intention of walking through the doorway but found herself slipping quietly through the narrow gap and standing in a small passageway. She started walking. The building reeked of disuse. It was made up of narrow corridors and stairs. Every so often, a corridor opened out into a courtyard with small rooms around it. Seemingly at random, some of these rooms also had doors that led to yet another courtyard. Each one was open to the sky with a moon that wavered above. There was soil beneath Fatima's bare feet and the old planted gardens, now grown wayward, were home to fig and olive trees.

It was as she entered one of these open courtyards that she unexpectedly found the man to whom the voice belonged. There was something familiar about him – a familiarity that led her to slowly walk towards him with arms outstretched. As the two embraced, she found herself full of desire. She wanted to take him in and delicately savour him. She felt as if she was turning herself inside out so that her vulva formed a canopy above the sky and the swaying moon. All night she loved him and, as the dawn broke, spreading a faint watery light, she retracted and gently spat him out like the stone of an olive.

As her dream continued, the streets came to life. Mules started to bray even though the morning was still fragile. The sun climbed higher in the sky. Nesting storks rose, dreamily, from the pink ramparts. A starving kitten forgot hunger for a moment and played in the blueness of the scattered flowers of a jacaranda tree. The orange blossoms and bougainvillea breathed in the damp before the rising fumes of dust and petrol filled the air.

The next morning, Fatima leaned on the sink watching the cat, who lolled apathetically by the side of a crimson geranium. July had finally paid heed to the forecasters, obliging with a heat previously rare in England. Each day had grown hotter and hotter. Only the flowers were active in the heat, frantic – besotted with their own need to propagate. Sun-stroked stamen quivered in their dreams of seed and soil.

The lethargy of her cats sometimes worried Fatima. They led a life totally lacking in development. She would have liked to enrol them on an Open University course or set them an unachievable goal, which they could spend their lives trying purposefully, yet fruitlessly, to achieve. But this wasn't possible so, instead, she tapped on the kitchen window to elicit some response. Salah heard. His ears twitched but he didn't turn. Fatima saw the twitching ears and was satisfied.

Abruptly closing the kitchen window, she decided to visit Lily again soon.

16

It had rained during the night in Warsaw. But Janina woke to a dazzling blue sky. The Warsaw streets had been steamed wet and clean, like a hot washhouse and, in the distance, the palace of culture – free from all aesthetic pretensions – shoved its clumsy head through the frail clouds. On the other side of the road, freshly laundered clothes, still scalding from the wash, hung expectantly on high-rise balconies. The strange hothouse blooms waited for a breeze, their limp, wet petals scaling the washing lines; dripping sleeves and trouser legs entwined like the stems of horizontal creepers.

Janina had her usual breakfast of two strong black coffees before her meeting with her client, Professor Kaminski. The meeting went without a hitch and she was able to sort out all of the queries that had been holding her up. She was glad that she hadn't cancelled the meeting. Professor Kaminski had put a lot of work her way over the years and it was good to take extra pains to please him. As it turned out, he also passed on some new work from a friend of his. It was a translation that had been gathering dust for some time by the looks of it, but financially it was a commission worth having.

The most unexpected part of her meeting with Professor Kaminski happened when they paused for a quick break, sauntering down to the coffee bar for a cup of espresso. Because they'd been working together, on and off, for some years, Janina and Professor Kaminski knew a number of things about each other's personal lives. She knew that his wife suffered from asthma and had a collection of teapots. She knew he had a dog that didn't like being taken for walks when it was raining. Professor Kaminski, in turn, knew a little bit about Janina's husband and two daughters.

They embarked on a bit of small talk on these subjects.

"How's your wife's asthma?" enquired Janina.

"Much the same as usual; it comes and goes," said Professor Kaminski. "And how are your lovely daughters? Lidka, named in keeping with her Polish heritage and Eve, so named because of her father's mountaineering interests."

Janina was nonplussed.

"What do you mean?" she asked.

It was true that Owen had named Eve. Janina had chosen the name Lidka for their eldest daughter, so it seemed only fair. She couldn't recall what, if any, explanation Owen had offered for his choice but she was sure she'd remember if it had been linked to crampons, thermal underwear or the possibility of altitude sickness. Owen had considered a series of names. The one immediately before Eve had been Consuela, a choice Janina hadn't warmed to. It didn't seem to suit a newborn baby. Owen had gone off the idea when a friend suggested, jokingly, that since they had no Spanish heritage, their daughter might go through life being accused of cultural appropriation. When Consuela was replaced by Eve, Janina had jumped at it without debate.

Professor Kaminski shrugged at Janina's question.

"I presumed," he said, pausing with his cup of espresso in his hand, "that because your surname is Reston, Eve had been so called so that her full name spelt Everest – with 'on' at the end because that is where your husband would, presumably, like to be. On Everest."

Janina stared at Professor Kaminski in silence, taking this information in.

"It is my understanding," continued Professor Kaminski to fill Janina's silence, "that Sir George Everest, Surveyor General of India, whom the mountain was named after always pronounced his name *Eve-rest* rather than the mispronunciation that people have adopted for the peak."

Janina drained her espresso.

"Yes," she said. "I expect some people might consider it an unusual idea. But it's typical of Owen."

She was sure that Professor Kaminski was correct. It was infuriating that she'd had to wait seven years – and travel to Poland – to discover that her own daughter was named in honour of a mountain. She was also certain that Owen had deliberately withheld from her his reason for choosing this name.

After the meeting with Professor Kaminski, Janina made her way to the restaurant where she'd arranged to meet Franz. She wasn't at all sure whether this lunchtime engagement was a good idea. If she'd been on friendlier terms with Owen before her departure from England, she'd have told him about it. Because they'd not been living together, the opportunity hadn't come up and, in the circumstances, it wouldn't have seemed appropriate.

"Time's a great healer," Zosia had said to Janina when Franz dumped her, and that had been true. She'd no feelings for him now – at least, not positive ones. Underneath, the way he'd treated her still rankled. This was why she'd agreed to meet him. It was a challenge to herself. To not meet him would have been an admission of defeat.

She made sure she was a good ten minutes late, even though the delay added to her own anxiety. She was annoyed to discover that she'd still arrived before him. She wasn't sure she'd recognise him but there was no one belonging to the right age group and nobody raised questioning eyes as she walked in.

She chose a table which was near enough to the door so that anyone coming in could see her but which was not close enough to make their approach too easy. She looked through the menu and wondered whether she should order. Should she wait for Franz? She decided to go ahead. She was glad she did. It made the food seem the primary reason for being there and relegated the meeting with Franz to a secondary purpose. Her anxiety at meeting him was gradually replaced by irritation at the thought that he wouldn't turn up at all. Worse still, perhaps he'd turn up so embarrassingly late that she'd be relieved to see him and the relief would be there for him to notice.

Janina wished Gladys was there to chat with but, of course, she wasn't. She was still where Janina had left her in her haste to get out of the family home after finding her ruined dress in the wardrobe. She was probably busy building an invisible web inside the bathroom cabinet, completely oblivious to Janina's predicament.

Janina had first met Franz when he'd come to live in London. He'd arranged to stay with his sister – Janina's friend – for the first few weeks, while he looked for a place of his own. Janina's friend was away when he was due to arrive and Janina agreed to meet him from the station. He said that he'd carry a bunch of red roses so that she'd recognise him. It seemed a poetic thing for a physicist to be carrying on a cold, windswept station. Her heart had warmed to him before they met. They'd slept together that first night.

"You've got cold feet," he'd whispered, his toes touching hers under the bed covers; her fingers nervously touching him, gathering flowers of pleasure from pale goose pimpled flesh.

"It's too late for cold feet now," he'd said.

He was older than her and seemed infallible. Only when he slept did he seem vulnerable. There was something about his vulnerability in sleep that she liked. After a few months, he'd gone – moved in with another woman. The other woman was much older than Janina – much older even than Franz himself – and much wiser and more politically sophisticated than her.

After Franz left, she discovered she was pregnant. She was too proud to tell him; too humiliated to tell her parents. She thought of having an abortion but had lost the baby anyway. It was easy to think that she'd willed the miscarriage. She felt a sense of termination in her own life as well. She woke each morning with no sense of pleasure or motivation. She immersed herself in her studies, slowly teaching herself how to care again. She had a number of other relationships, and then she met Owen.

Janina thought of her parents in their kitchen. Were all relationships a case of mistaken identity; a hopeless tangle of confused expectations; a squeezing out of souls into cold, dirty washing up water?

The golonka she'd chosen for her main course was delicious. The pork knuckle had been slowly cooked to a pink and honeyed tenderness, its sauce glazing the perfectly seasoned cabbage and potatoes. As she progressed onto ice cream, her frame of mind shifted and she no longer felt affronted by the non-appearance of her ex-lover. She felt neither disappointed nor pleased; it was inconsequential. If he contacted her to apologise and to ask to meet up, she'd be able to decline in the full knowledge that it was because she didn't care to see him rather than because she had feelings she wanted to avoid.

She congratulated the waiter on the quality of the food and, as she walked away from the restaurant, she was only half-aware of a tall, slightly greying man hurrying towards it. It was a minute later that she realised who the man was and was pleased that she'd left when she did. A direct meeting with him would have been tiresome.

Janina turned the word 'tiresome' over in her head several times, and liked it. She sang a little as she walked back to her hotel.

17

It could have been strange forces, activated by a string of mystic happenings, that resulted in the changing architectural structure of Lily's home and the incursion of forest into her dining room. However, for some time before his death, Ernest had been concerned about large patches of damp on the inside wall and areas of crumbling brick on the outside. He'd also raised doubts about the aptitude and application of the builders who'd installed the patio doors.

The growth of a tropical and sub-tropical forest could be harder to explain. Although, in the late 1800s, shortly after the first phase of the park that sat at the bottom of Lily's garden was opened to the public, an extra area of land had been added. Under the direction of the chief planning officer of the time, it had been used for planting species of tropical and sub-tropical flora. It was a personal obsession of that particular planning officer, and he'd ensured an impressive range and variety of lush vegetation were planted. Trees, shrubs and flowers had all been seeded and saplings interred in their new home. At first, there'd been eager public interest but then it had waned, giving way to the lure of the more modern pleasures of the boating lake and lido.

In the 1950s and 60s, children's fixed play structures had been added along with an aviary and a small zoo, housing reptiles and birds. At that time, a 'parkie' patrolled the municipal grounds. He ruled the urban greenery with a firm hand. His small team of assistants mended the fences and fed the animals. But, over the decades, pressure from central government on local authority spending had worked its own not-so-mystical outcomes. The park keeper and his team were enchanted out of existence by council restructures and a negative form of alchemy turned the base metal of the fences around the animal enclosures into gaping air.

In recent years, the city council had decided to sell one large tract of parkland, too compacted by strange vegetation to be of use to even the most intrepid dog walker. It was to be cleared and the land used to build new homes. The area was fenced off so there was no longer access from the park. Then, at the last minute, it was discovered that it couldn't be used for redevelopment. It was documented, in black and white. It belonged to the people of the city for their leisure and recreational use only.

The fences remained. The alien trees and flowers crept over the grass, spreading their twilight, unnoticed, until the unusually hot summer stirred the slurried depths of their past, transporting the trees and flowers back to the wilder spaces of their sap-driven memories. Dreaming of faraway places, a new pulse beat within their green chloroplasts – wanderlust and desire hurried their advance. It set them peeping over Lily's broken fence, leaning on crumbling brick that flinched, then welcomed their exotic touch.

18

Being adept in mathematics and arithmetical skills, Janina would have been able to calculate the cost of Lily's trip to the seaside as a percentage of the cost of her own return flight to Warsaw. The personal effect of the trip to Poland on Janina wasn't quite as dramatic as the result of Lily's trip to the seaside. Assessed in this way, Lily's excursion was cost-effective compared to Janina's. But Janina's visit to Poland and its revelations had, at least, crystallised the knowledge that she had to do something soon about her relationship with Owen.

On the plane journey home, Janina decided that when she picked up the girls and took them home, she would stay as well. She was missing her daughters very much and she couldn't put upon Celia's hospitality forever.

"I've bought you a wardrobe," Owen said, dramatically, when Janina phoned him from Zosia's.

"Really?" she said. She couldn't bring herself to say 'thank you'. After all, it was only right that Owen had provided the space.

When she arrived, Owen made an effort to welcome her. He told her all the details of his climbing trip, cooked tea and then ran her a bath. She decided that the confrontation over Eve's name could wait a little. After such a long time it was difficult to know how to approach the subject.

Janina lay in the bath full of bubbles that had emerged from a pink plastic bottle with a gold cork. She reclined up to her neck in the warm water, sipping a glass of wine. The wine bottle was on the floor in a position that Owen had designated as not a threat to human safety. Two candles flickered in a silver candlestick on the windowsill. She wasn't usually prone to displays of attempted decadence but she was celebrating a victory, so it seemed fitting. The victory, however, was limited.

She'd expected Owen to make a few sacrifices. She'd anticipated that he'd throw out some of his own threadbare garments to redress the balance and make sure she got more of the existing space. Instead he'd gone out and bought an extra wardrobe, into which some of his own clothes were already overflowing. Her own garments were no longer crumpled but the issue, she now realised, had never been about clothes but about equality. Creased fabric had only been a symbol of inequality. Janina believed that power was finite and a bit of empowering here necessitated a bit of relinquishing of power there. The purchase of the new wardrobe was evidence that Owen didn't subscribe to the same concept of power at all.

The new item of furniture didn't even have any aesthetic qualities to recommend it and it took up more space in the bedroom. They had to open the bedroom door carefully now so it didn't bang against it. In addition, Janina, who slept at the far side of the bed, had to squeeze through the narrow gap left between the end of the bed and the dressing table, which had had to be repositioned to make room for the wardrobe. When she'd raised this as a possible health and safety contravention, Owen told her it wasn't a problem. He'd already carried out a risk assessment and she could safely climb over the bed if necessary.

"If I insist on a continuing move to domestic equality," said Janina to Gladys, "we'll end up living like canned sardines or have to move to a larger house."

Gladys was quick to point out that even moving house was unlikely to solve the problem. The whole process would just start again with the same end result. They would have to keep moving to bigger and bigger houses.

Janina was sure this was true. If all women insisted on having as much space as men, the last few wildernesses of the world would soon be gobbled up by male resistance to making concessions. Finally, the whole planet would implode. The debris of empowerment would scatter through the galaxy. Shattered storage solutions would orbit Mars, collide with shooting stars and venture to parts of the galaxy that no item of household furniture had ever been before.

There was another issue. Janina wasn't sure she wanted a pet parrot or whether she really wished to master the art of belly dancing, as she'd suggested to Owen. But Owen had ringed – in bold red felt pen – two advertisements in the local paper. She would have to show some interest in them or Owen might think she hadn't been serious about the wardrobe. This would result in a more energetic incursion into her new hanging space.

She blew a soap bubble away from the classifieds and read the two adverts Owen had highlighted.

The first said:

Parrots and other exotic birds. Phone Lily…

And the second one stated:

For expert belly dancing tuition from Shaz, contact the Queen's Head…

She dried herself and got into bed. Owen was already asleep so she leafed through the translation from Professor Kaminski's friend. It was a historical text about Vladimir Lenin's personal life. Most of it was incredibly dry. It might have been interesting many years ago but now it seemed obsolete, a relic from another century. The most intriguing bits were about his sexual liaisons. The writer was female and Janina wondered whether she, or one of her ancestors, had an affair with him. Had she been Lenin's lover?

She read only a few pages of the document before starting to yawn. She turned off the bedside light and was soon asleep.

It wasn't particularly surprising that Lenin was mixed up with the subject of her dream. She was in bed with Owen which, of course, was true in reality as well.

"Let's pretend that you're Lenin and that I'm one of his female comrades," said Janina in the dream.

"I'm not some dead Communist," said Owen.

Janina half woke with annoyance and in this state of semi-consciousness was able to restart the dream to see if it could have a more favourable outcome the second time round.

"Let's pretend you're Lenin and I'm your very attractive female comrade called Alexandra," she tried this time.

"Okay," said Owen.

"Leninism is a bourgeois notion derived from the auto-cratic social structures of the former Tsarist regime," said Alexandra, sitting in an erotic position on top of Lenin.

"I agree," said Lenin.

"You can't," said Alexandra. "You're supposed to argue. You're Lenin. You were all for Leninism the last time we met in 1918."

"I'm Lenin," said Lenin. "I can say what the fuck I like."

Not for the first time, Alexandra woke up feeling decidedly annoyed with her male comrades. She glanced at Owen. She was finding it difficult to separate the Owen in the dream from the Owen beside her. He was in a deep sleep and probably dreaming his own dreams. She reclaimed a few more centimetres of duvet. She knew she was going to have to give these women, Lily and Shaz the belly dancer, a ring.

She looked at Owen again and wondered what he dreamt about. Were men's dreams different to women's? What would she dream if she were a man?

19

As Janina was reclaiming the duvet from Owen, Bill Gupta was dreaming that he was in a large department store. It was a House of Fraser of social relationships. Each department had a familiar name such as stationery, electrical goods and soft furnishings but, instead of containing the usual merchandise, they were inhabited by people. The department you found yourself in was symbolic of the sort of social interaction that characterised your life.

Bill found himself inexorably placed in the haberdashery department. He tried to escape to the mouth-watering delights of the food hall, to the racy voluptuousness of the personal apparel and the heady pleasures of perfumery but each attempt was thwarted by vigilant staff in blue gingham blouses. As he awoke, he was making a last bid escape down the escalator to the sensible and stable security of the DIY corner. But even as he opened his eyes, he could feel the hot breath of the store detective on his neck.

So it was that Bill believed that his capacity for establishing friendships was stuck forever in the haberdashery department of human relationships. It wasn't a good way to start a new day.

The day after having the dream about the haberdashery department, Bill went for a drink in the Queen's Head.

"What do they sell in a haberdashery department?" Bill asked Alex, the barman. The phone rang while Alex was still pondering the question. It was Janina.

"Belly dancing? That'll be Shaz. If you phone back in a few days, I'll be able to give you her new mobile number," said Alex. Then, as a favour to Bill, he asked: "Do you know what they sell in a haberdashery department?"

There was a moment's silence at the other end of the phone.

"Bric-a-brac," Janina said, after giving the subject some thought.

"Bric-a-brac," said Alex, putting the phone down and turning back to Bill. Bill looked blankly at Alex. Alex shrugged his shoulders.

"Have you got any phobias?" Bill asked, thinking of Myrta.

"Not really," said Alex. "How about you?"

"Cats," said Bill, as Alex refilled a customer's pint glass. "Hamsters make much better pets. I've just got a new one."

Bill had gone out for a while with a girl who worked in a small mammal rescue centre. He adopted one of her hamsters. He'd thought that by doing so, she might rescue him, even though he was a much larger mammal than those she usually took pity on. The relationship had come to an end but he'd kept the hamster. He'd grown fond of her and called her Amelia. Just before he'd moved out of his flat, Amelia had got out of her cage. His landlady was unsympathetic.

"Those vermin get into the pipes. They burrow under the floorboards and run riot behind the walls," she said when Bill told her. "They eat the house."

"How can a hamster eat a house?" Bill had asked.

"You'd be surprised," said his landlady.

What Bill feared was that Myrta had eaten his hamster.

Occasionally, Bill had the sensation that his whole life was empty. In reality he knew that it wasn't because he could hear a dull thud, thud from inside, which meant there must be something in there. A loss, however, should always be replaced. Otherwise emptiness could start to invade. When he was sure his lost hamster wasn't coming back, he'd bought another. He called his new pet Amelia the Second.

"I'm not keen on snakes," said Alex, wiping the bar. "But it's not really a phobia. My gran had a cousin who emigrated to Australia. He had his leg bitten off by a crocodile."

He paused, at a loss as to why he'd introduced the bit about the crocodile. "That wasn't a phobia though either. He'd have been better off if he'd had a phobia of reptiles. Might have kept his distance."

"And kept his leg," said Bill, draining his pint.

The flat where Bill was temporarily living was a high-rise on the edge of a trendy neighbourhood. It had been redeveloped along a section of the derelict banks of the canal. It didn't take Bill long to walk there from the Queen's Head. He sat on the sofa in front of the huge TV. He felt tired. The dream about the department store of social relationships had disturbed his sleep the night before. He went to bed.

He liked to sleep with the curtains open, especially if the night was clear. It was a full moon. The air conditioning, set far too high, continued its not quite subliminal hum.

He pulled the duvet tight around him but still couldn't get warm. Eventually, he dragged himself out of bed to turn the air conditioning down.

Wide awake, he walked through to the kitchen, taking Amelia the Second out of her cage and popping her onto his shoulder on the way. He could see the city spread out below him – people's plans and hopes expressed as neon trails as they drove along the urban roads. There were no stars visible in the orange sky, just the jaundiced moon that looked down on the towpath along the embankment. One or two dark shapes wavered by the old brick bridge; homeless shadows or people who had forgotten where home was.

"Bric-a-brac," said Bill to his hamster despondently. It was worse than he'd thought.

"Have you made any of those meaningful changes to your life yet?" Owen asked Janina nicely as they got ready for bed. Apart from phoning the Queen's Head, Janina had spent the day clearing a backlog of ironing and cleaning the house.

She took out an English dictionary, which she kept with some foreign language dictionaries in the dressing table.

"Yes," she said. She wanted to check the definition of haberdashery. It was playing on her mind.

She squeezed past the bottom of the bed, running her finger down the page past *haar: a cold sea fog; Hab: an abbreviation for the prophet Habakkuk; habanera: a slow Cuban dance with two beats to the bar.*

She drew the curtains.

Habeas corpus: investigations into the lawfulness of someone's restraint.

It seemed distinctly cooler and a thin mist was turning into rain.

20

Shortly after Janina had gone to bed, and after Bill and Amelia had gazed out at the city beneath them, rumbles of thunder shook the clouds as the tension of elements – resisting change – relaxed into the inevitability of new formations. Rearranged molecules strung across space in microscopic chains collided in the skies, embracing in soft liaisons. They fell to earth, reshaping the backs of unwary cats into rain-splattered concaves. Rivulets of shadow splashed off rooftops on quiet paws in search of shelter.

It was still raining the next morning. Violet meowed to go out but when Fatima opened the door, a cold driving wetness seeped into the house. Violet took one look and one sniff at the dripping garden then arched her back, treading shiftily backwards from the damp. She made her way, instead, to the shop door and meowed again noisily. Fatima knew that Violet wouldn't go out, so she avoided going through the motions until the incessant meowing became too much, and she finally relented. She opened the door just a crack. Violet rubbed past her legs to squeeze through the narrow gap but, as the wet spattered onto her paws, she drew back in surprise and went to sit on the windowsill instead.

Violet's philosophy of different doors leading to different universes was an interesting one, thought Fatima. Today, as on many other days, all universes – or all doors – had conspired against them.

While she and Violet were exchanging depressed glances, the phone rang.

"I'm doing some cooking," said Lily. "I'm making guava jam, pudding fruit ice cream and sugar-apple flummery. Would you like to come over?"

When Fatima arrived, Lily was stirring fruit in a saucepan and keeping an eye on Václav Havel. Václav had been acting strangely.

Lily knew from her studies that when he was made president, Václav Havel had refused to live in Prague Palace. He opted to live in a flat on the right bank of the river. She couldn't help thinking that the palace would have been a much better place for Václav to live. It was bound to be full of mice. She could imagine Václav having a wonderful time chasing them down the corridors. But Lily had been having a strange dream. Because of his odd behaviour, she couldn't help wondering whether Václav had experienced it too.

In the dream, Václav was the only cat in what was really a dog show. It was a particularly odd dream because everything was viewed from Václav's perspective, as if she was seeing the world through the cat's eyes. Václav didn't know how he'd come to be in a dog show but he was the star turn. His fur had become long and fluffy, a bit like a Persian cat, and he had to walk from one tall stool along a thin metal bar to another about 20 metres away. First, he had to do this on his own. Then the trainer had put a little hamster on his back. The hamster climbed all over him while he was walking. Václav wasn't allowed to shake the hamster off. He knew that if he tried to, the trainer would do something terrible to him. Later, the trainer placed the hamster halfway along the bar and Václav had to carefully step over her on his way from one stool to the other.

In the beginning, Václav wanted to grab the hamster with his paws but after a while a friendship grew between them. He discovered that the hamster's name was Amelia and, without the trainer realising, they were able to communicate with each other and formulate a plan. They would subvert the act. They would go through the act, in the normal way, but at the end, when the trainer placed the hamster on Václav's head, they would commit the most devastatingly subversive act that they could think of – Václav would eat Amelia.

Afterwards, Václav couldn't remember whose idea it had been in the first place. Had it been his idea or had Amelia first thought of it? All he could remember was the feeling of horror as he crunched the hamster's bones. What if Amelia had changed her mind about the plan at the last minute when it was too late to say? And why had they thought it would be a triumph? In the dream, Václav was left with very confused feelings towards hamsters and Lily was left feeling confused as to whose dream it had been.

As she stepped from the cool, watery street through Lily's front door, Fatima was aware that a mixture of luscious, mouth-watering smells pervaded the house. She breathed in deeply, trying to identify some of them. Syrup, sherbet and chocolate were layered and dissected by fresh lemon and strawberry; sweet and fruity.

Václav made a wary retreat to his favourite bonsai tree.

"I've got a forest growing in my dining room," Lily told Fatima, matter-of-factly.

"Well, houseplants can get a bit out of hand," said Fatima.

"No," said Lily, pausing to gather her thoughts, "that's not what I mean. I'll show you later. I'm just making the guava jam."

"Can you carry on stirring?" Lily asked Fatima. "Then I can do some more chopping."

Lily had baskets of fruit strewn around the kitchen, overflowing onto the work surfaces. From the pile of light yellow-skinned and green pear-like fruits, she selected the ones she wanted. She sliced through the first with a large knife, revealing white flesh inside. The next exposed an inner pink and the third a dark red centre. A sweet musky odour seeped out as she cut into the soft skin.

"I love guava," said Fatima.

Lily passed Fatima a piece of dissected fruit. "If you carry on stirring the jam," she said, as the flavour of strawberry and pear invaded Fatima's mouth. "I'll see to the sugar-apple flummery."

Lily picked up a large creamy yellow heart-shaped fruit and placed it on her chopping board.

"I've collected all these from the forest," she said by means of explanation. "This fruit's known as custard apple. I prefer its other name of sugar-apple. It tastes like straw-berries and cream. They originate from the mountainous region between Colombia, Bolivia and Ecuador but this one grew ten feet away from the patio doors. The tree they grow on is sometimes known as 'the tree of ice cream'."

Fatima continued stirring. The sweet toffee-like smell hung in the air and Lily's words gave the whole morning an almost tangible sense of unreality.

Lily started whipping cream until it was thick. Then she squeezed juice from the sugar-apple and added it, deftly blending the two ingredients together with a wooden spoon.

"Could you get the ice cream out?" she asked. "I'll get the chilled lemon tea and we can have our picnic."

"This isn't a picnic, it's a feast," said Fatima. The word feast ended in a squeak of surprise as a beautifully plumaged parrot flew into the kitchen and landed on Lily's arm – stealing a piece of guava from her fingers.

"Lolita! I've told you about stealing," said Lily.

"I've told you about stealing," repeated the parrot, looking accusingly at Fatima, who was holding the dish of ice cream.

"That parrot has no manners," said Lily apologetically, as Lolita flew off again. "Shall we eat outside?"

"It's a bit on the cool side," said Fatima.

"Not out there, it isn't," said Lily, nodding in the direction in which the parrot had flown. "Come on."

Lily took Fatima through to the dining room. Fatima stared at the green light and the warmth emanating from what looked like a big open doorway. Lily beckoned her in. Fatima had always been afraid of forests. She sensed that something lurked behind the trunks of the trees – a presence that might reach out and grab her from just beyond the thin veil of green foliage. She paused on the threshold, torn between inquisitiveness and fear. She took a deep breath.

"Come on," said Lily. "The ice cream will melt."

Fatima stepped into the hothouse heat through the creeper-strewn gap where the patio doors used to be. She wondered whether the rain had stopped and the sun emerged while she and Lily had been in the kitchen – or whether Violet's philosophies on different doors had been right after all. How odd to have her beliefs proved incorrect by her cat.

A bird that sounded like a peacock cried from a long way off.

Fatima was wearing trousers and trainers. It was just as well, for the ground, as Lily had feared, soon became spongy as they entered the wood by way of a shady archway of intertwined trees. Neither Fatima nor Lily could see any animals, though little scurrying noises could be heard from the undergrowth and from the leafy canopy above their heads. Creepers climbed up the thick grey trunks of the trees and the women could hear the cry of exotic sounding birds.

They were both quiet. Every now and then, Fatima gave an excited exclamation as she spotted unusual blooms. Soon, it was hard to tell how far they'd walked or for how long.

"Where are we?" asked Fatima.

"I don't know," said Lily. "I've no idea how big the forest is or what's on the other side."

The two women sauntered a little way along the gently sun-striped ground. Dappled light trickled through the musky canopy, sliding down gnarled trunks to flicker patterns around their feet and ankles. The heat was soothing, the air shimmering with iridescent colour. There was an occasional soft exclamation of muted sound, as if the air encapsulated pockets of half-forgotten summer memories. The almost-captured recollections distilled like a perfume and textured the forest. Fatima thought she sensed, rather than saw, the hovering form of a hummingbird but she couldn't be sure. When the trees thinned into a small clearing, the women decided to sit down and unpack the picnic.

They ate, absorbed in their own thoughts. Lily was starting to realise that allowing a forest to grow in her home could have even bigger implications than she'd first thought. The forest that had entered her home stretched further than her garden or, indeed, her neighbourhood. Things that lived in the forest – perhaps even things that lived at the other side of it – might enter her personal living space. So far, Lolita, who Lily had become quite fond of – despite her bad manners – had been the only living creature to arrive, but Lily had a feeling that it was only a matter of time before other things, perhaps other people, wandered out of the trees and into her life.

21

The same week that Lily embarked on her ice cream making and jam production, Janina had also been thinking about doing some cooking. It was a subject she thought about sometimes, but she rarely got round to the practicalities of cooking something new. That evening she'd been toying with the idea of making an ancient Arabic dish that she'd discovered in a script she'd recently translated. Would the local butcher stock a sheep's head?

Janina believed that if there was a god, and if it materialised in human form, it would appear as a woman in a grubby apron. She would have streaks of flour in her hair as she gleefully measured ingredients on a pair of celestial scales. The scales meant that numbers would play an essential part, along with the ingredients and the heat, in forging magnificent chemical changes. Numbers would not be abstract but living; always attached to something, flitting from one ingredient to another like a bee collecting pollen. They'd buzz here and there – always with a purpose, always recycled – never wearing out or growing old.

What power the cook of creation would have; altering atoms, changing solids to gases and transforming gases to liquid. She would experiment with the properties of things that seemed unchangeable, porous to non-porous, malleable to non-malleable. The kitchen would be full of aromatic smells. Clouds of warmly spiced air would float above a washing up bowl of dirty cooking utensils, waiting in the soapy suds to be cleaned so the cycle could start again.

In the end, Janina decided it was too hot to have the oven on for a long time and opted to make omelettes instead. It was surprising how much washing up was generated even from eating quickly prepared food. She was washing the dishes and watching Owen and the girls. They were attempting to construct a tent in the back garden. It didn't appear to be going too well.

"It looks like a cuboid formed from regular isosceles triangles," shouted Janina helpfully, through the open window.

Distracted for a moment, Owen hit his finger with the hammer he was using to secure a peg in the ground. One canvas isosceles triangle gave up its perpendicular properties and flopped onto Eve's head.

"Nomadic peoples of Asia have lived in tents like that for hundreds of years. They call them yurts," continued Janina. "Apparently they're now taken very seriously as a form of modern living space."

Another isosceles triangle became a horizontal representation of three interconnected planes. It marked out its mathematical statement in waterproof fabric against the scorched lawn. Owen gave Janina a look.

"I'm popping down to the Queen's Head," she said. "There's someone I need to see."

Owen muttered something under his breath that Janina didn't catch. She paused in the doorway, waiting to see if he would repeat it but he didn't.

Janina's two ginger cats, Gus and Carlotta, bored with observing the whole tent fiasco, followed Janina down the street. Gus wound around her legs, almost tripping her up as she walked, while Carlotta sauntered behind, distracted by noises beyond human hearing. Gus sat down without warning and started to wash, as if – in a split second – he'd lost interest or was prevented from going further by an unwritten regulation known only to cats. Carlotta, flouting feline bylaws, continued shadowing Janina a little further. For some reason, they'd presumed she was a tom when they'd first got her and called her Carl. The name Carlotta suited her. If Carlotta had been a human, she would have worn an orange crinoline and been pursued, insistently and amorously (though historically inconsistently), by men out of Jane Austen novels.

Carlotta blinked her clear blue eyes, feigning a fainting spell on the dusty pavement. Ignoring her, Janina decided to visit Bill Gupta. She'd call in at the pub to find out about the belly dancing later. She needed to see his sister, Gertie, whom Bill had introduced her to a few days earlier. She'd asked Janina to do some translations of Russian poetry written by a women's group in Moscow. Gertie wanted to share the poems (translated into Urdu) with an Asian women's group that she ran. When Janina arrived, Gertie was out so Janina had a cup of tea with Bill and they caught up on each other's latest news.

The windows of Bill's house were wide open and the sounds of summer drifted in on the light breeze – the gentle buzz of a lawn mower, the distant music of an ice cream van (always and forever six streets away), someone calling, children running, a bird singing. A whole collection of encapsulated sounds forming a bridge from the present to the past. It was a link too delicate to sustain and, no sooner perceived, than it was already accompanied by a sense of loss – like soap bubbles blown into the air to be fractured into non-existence at the very moment of their capture.

"What do you think love is?" Janina asked Bill, lulled into a philosophical mood by the motes of sunlight playing in the air. Janina wasn't sure whether love was an extreme level of liking or whether, as a friend had once suggested, you could love someone deeply without actually liking them much at all.

"Sometimes," said Bill, approaching the question from an obtuse angle. "I'm not at all sure what it is you want from me."

"Never to presume anything about me," said Janina, the answer appearing from nowhere before she'd had time to think of it.

She got up, suddenly surprised and restless. She looked out of the window, beyond the muslin curtains, at Bill's washing hanging on the line. She thought about Owen's shrunken jumper. Everything had been slightly different since then, as if there'd been some shift in her mind. Bill's garments hung, colour coded; each piece of clothing advancing through the colours of the rainbow – yellow boxer shorts, green shirt, blue jeans. They sagged, motionless, in the resonant evening warmth. A spectrum of colour, strung out from the wall of the house to the shed, where dragonflies buzzed above a blue water butt, its contents turned gold by the sinking sun.

"You can tell a lot about someone," said Janina, "from the way they hang their washing on the line."

22

The Queen's Head had never served food and, as far as Alex – the landlord – was concerned, it never would. However, since Shaz set up her belly dancing classes in the church opposite, she and her students had come in each week afterwards demanding food. Alex had placated them by raiding his own fridge and cooking for them on his own cooker in the upstairs flat. Once started, the custom just carried on. Alex didn't mind, after all Shaz had introduced a group of new customers so, when Janina came in, he obligingly passed over Shaz's new number.

Outside the Queen's Head, it was still warm. The heat of the day trapped between drooping sky and parched pavement. Walking further from the centre of the city and down the streets that led to her house, Janina tried calling Shaz's number but there was no reply. The roads were almost deserted, only a few cats wandered; some feline purpose intrinsic to each of their fluent movements. Janina wondered if Jasper, the obnoxious socio-biologist, would ever write a feline social and political demography of the city. It would be a new approach to urban geography.

It would look at the city's existence as if it was a body that created a shadow. Cats were part of the solidity but also part of the shadow. They slipped through their owners' cat-flapped consciousness and into their dreams, moving stealthily through shadow and light – domesticity and freedom – picking paths through urban jungles, regardless of ownership and rights. There was no part of the city that was free from them. Only their names varied, depending on the section of the urban landscape from which they came. Jasper's account could have a historical perspective:

The redeveloped middle-class areas of the inner-city breed cats named Barnabas and Gandalf. The monetarist nineties drove out the Smudges and Snowys to the lower middle-class estates on the edge of town, and out further still to the working-class boroughs. Only cats named after the latest football stars are in every part of the city. They are as classless as unrequited love and clandestine McChicken sandwiches on a Saturday night.

But, of course, Jasper would never write this because it would no longer be socio-biology.

All was quiet as Janina let herself into the house. She found Owen in the kitchen. After doing virtually no household chores for some weeks, he'd suddenly decided that all the work surfaces needed thoroughly disinfecting.

"How did it go with the tent?" Janina asked.

"Your mother phoned," he replied rather loudly, as if the smell of bleach was an invasive noise.

He didn't impart any further information about the call but there was something weighty in the silence that followed, and in the way he stood with the cloth poised in his hand, that invited further enquiry from Janina.

"What did she want?" she asked.

"She's divorcing your father," said Owen. He imparted the news in an annoyingly matter of fact tone.

Janina ran through an ad hoc selection of Eastern European and ancient Arabic expletives in her head. She switched on the kettle and picked up a mug, sniffing it suspiciously. It was as she thought – Owen had a habit of bleaching the mugs and then not rinsing them sufficiently. She went off the idea of a cup of tea and took a can of lemonade from the fridge instead. She tugged the ring pull in one decisive motion.

"Have you ever heard of anyone naming a child after a mountain?" she asked, as if the spluttering of the lemonade had imbued the subject with sudden urgency.

"What?" asked Owen.

Janina watched the frothing bubbles as they hissed around the top of the can and then subsided.

"I'll go and see Mum in the morning," she said.

She took a few gulps of lemonade then put the can down next to the draining board, leaving a sticky ring of carbonated sugar. The sucrose sizzled as it reacted to the diluted bleach on the work surface.

When Janina reached her parents' house, Zosia was sitting in the kitchen and Robert was at the bottom of the garden. They were both in identical positions to the ones they'd been in when Janina had left for Poland. Zosia looked a bit pink about the eyes. If she'd phoned the previous evening with an urge to confide her troubles, the impulse had passed overnight. Janina found her uncommunicative – a situation that she, guiltily, felt rather relieved about. Zosia was stitching her latest embroidery project. The fabric was a striking purple and she was using gold and silver thread. It looked huge and Janina couldn't think where her mother might be thinking of hanging it once it was complete.

"Ask your father," was all Zosia would say when, after twenty minutes of half-hearted small talk, Janina had broached the subject of her parents' difficulties.

Janina wandered down the garden path to see if Robert could throw any further light on the matter. As she reluctantly approached him, she thought about the conversation she might have with Owen later that day.

"Something important was happening in their lives yet they were in exactly the same position I'd left them in weeks ago," Janina imagined herself saying. "They hadn't moved, not even an inch, in physical space."

"What were you expecting?" Owen would say, "your mother to be hanging from the light shade and your father perched on top of his garden shed?"

Typical Owen comment, Janina thought in annoyance as she reached Robert.

"How's it going Dad?" she asked.

Robert was examining his apple trees. They were his only other hobby apart from his collection of souls and his diary writing. The trees were thick with blossom and later in the year, as always, the boughs would creak in the cooling autumn breeze, ready to snap with their overload of fruit. Perhaps it was the souls her father poached from his unsuspecting neighbours that evaporated into the air and breathed such vibrant life into the trees.

"Snails," said Robert to Janina, by way of greeting. "Hundreds of the little blighters."

He beckoned her over to have a look. Robert was right, the branches were full of them. She leaned in closer, amazed at how many there were and their colours. They were striped in all hues of green and gold and yellow. Their sticky secretions suckered them to the waxy, grey branches. Some were creeping slowly, weaving shiny tracks like mysterious messages in secreted code along the bark. If she looked at them closely, she could see their delicate antennae testing the conditions of each centimetre of the world before they edged into it.

"Where've they all come from?" asked Janina.

"Search me," said Robert.

"They're quite beautiful when you look at them closely," said Janina.

Robert was picking them off, one by one, and placing them in an old washing-up bowl. His large fingers closed around their delicate shells before hoisting them through the air, breaking the suction between the two life forms of tree and snail. Some of the snails were still at the bottom of the bowl where they'd retreated into their shells – startled into a denial of their situation. Others were sliding their silver white trails along the alien terrain of dead plastic, scaling the smooth featureless landscape of the bowl.

"Little buggers all the same," said Robert.

"Are you and Mum alright?" Janina ventured, as she heard the timer on the water spray in the next-door garden click into action and then the just discernible sound of thousands of fine water droplets landing on thirsty grass.

The question seemed out of context. It didn't fit with the conversation into which she inserted it. It didn't correspond with the nature of her usual relationship with her father. It felt unnatural to be enquiring after the health of her parents' relationship. It had always been the other way round – her parents enquiring after hers. That was the natural order of things. There was a substantial silence while Robert either pondered Janina's question or considered the garden's infestation of snails.

"We're much the same," said Robert.

"Are you sure?" asked Janina. "I don't think Mum's very happy."

"Isn't she?" said Robert, looking up for a moment, shading his eyes with an arm against the sun. "I wonder what that can be about."

23

Monica, granddaughter of the world-renowned Marlene, was sitting in her green and white deck chair on the promenade outside her fortune-telling establishment. She was reading, sneezing intermittently due to the excessively high pollen count. The copy of *La Chatte* by Colette was open at page twenty-four. A half-empty packet of chocolate digestives (which had melted rather badly in the sun) lay at her side, along with two empty glasses, which had contained generous measures of tequila. Monica was a great believer in eating while she read. Some story worlds gradually sweep you off your feet. It's a good idea to have a generous helping of chocolate pudding and custard before reading to increase personal gravity by a minimum of 700 calories of ballast to prevent you from being borne away forever.

However, in this instance, the ballast had been unnecessary. Monica had been on page twenty-four for some time. It wasn't because she found it any less readable than *Madame Bovary*, it was just that she had other things on her mind.

A few days earlier, Marlene – Monica's grandmother and proprietor of the Sea Witch B&B – had received a letter from Lily. The letter had thanked Marlene for the lovely break and the *Astro* magazines. Marlene had shown the letter to Monica who had, as planned, invested in a jar of tea granules to see if they would increase the accuracy of her teacup readings. Since receiving Lily's letter, Monica had experienced some extremely unusual results.

A clear picture of Lily had arisen from the gunge of

congealed granules at the bottom of her cup. It wasn't the same as the static patterns that usually appeared from tea leaves. While Monica gazed into the dregs, vivid moving images – as if from a dream sequence – had run through her head. It was this phenomenon which was disturbing her thoughts as she sat in her deck chair, the sun glittering on the calm sea.

The first vision had been of Lily herself. She was walking through a sub-tropical forest with a parrot on her shoulder. Monica guessed this meant Lily would be taking another holiday, this time to somewhere rather further afield than the English coast. The next vision had been more mysterious. The sequence of images had started with a group of women belly dancing, then switched to a woman wearing nothing but a primrose coloured towel and one Doc Marten boot. Then her mind was filled with a picture of a sand-bearing wind. The wind blew all the other images out of her head.

Monica tried to concentrate on *La Chatte*, reading the first sentence on page twenty-four for at least the tenth time. When she looked up, she saw a figure walking towards her.

Marlene often popped round in the afternoon after cooking her guest's breakfasts and cleaning their rooms, and before she started cooking the evening meal. Monica shook the biscuit crumbs out of her book, put the kettle on and told Marlene about her unusual visions. Marlene had a cup of granule tea then swished the dregs around expectantly. She stared into mid-air, transfixed by absolutely nothing for a couple of minutes to see whether she would experience similar cinematic images. Nothing happened, apart from Griselda, Monica's cat, suddenly materialising on the kitchen window ledge, causing both Monica and Marlene to jump. Griselda was the daughter of Houdini, who Marlene had adopted when he'd hitched a lift from the city on the back of a lorry to start a new life at the coast.

"Maybe you should note down what you see," said Marlene, washing the cups in the kitchen sink. "That might help get it out of your head and you can contact Lily and give her the details."

Griselda's appearance on the window ledge made Monica drop her bottle of anti-allergy medicine onto the work surface. It rolled noisily until stopping – label side up – against the bread bin.

One 5 ml spoonful, twice a day. Not to be taken with alcohol, the label warned. *May cause disturbances of vision.*

Monica sneezed twice then took another gulp from the bottle as Griselda wound her hot fur round her ankles.

"I've drunk gallons of this stuff," she said. "It doesn't seem to stop me sneezing. I've got through three bottles in the last three days. Fancy a tequila Nan?"

24

There was something terribly annoying about jumpers, Janina thought. They foisted themselves upon you in the shop, fluttering their labels. They made promises they had no intention of keeping and looked much nicer on the hanger than they did when you wore them. Once you'd washed them a few times, they mutated and shrank until they didn't resemble the jumper you'd originally bought at all.

She was trying to get a shop to take back a jumper she'd bought only a week and a half earlier. It had been an impulse buy, a spot of retail therapy, after the difficult visit to her parents. How friendly and helpful the shop assistants had been when she was buying it. Now it was a different matter. There were no smiles, no friendliness, and no chat, just the cold face of commerce. A contract had been entered into and the contract was binding. It made Janina feel cynical about the human race. Was it the same with friendships? What happened if people wouldn't accept the goods of emotional relationships back? What if they refused to refund emotions and dependencies?

Janina and the shop manager finally compromised with a gift voucher for the cost of the jumper. It had to be spent within six months. What would the equivalent exchange be on the termination of a romantic relationship, Janina wondered, as she drove home. A signed agreement to advise on stain removal for the following year? A written pact to give assistance in the moving of heavy items of furniture for the next three months?

When she reached her house, Robert was in the kitchen talking to Owen. This wasn't a good sign. Her father looked oddly out of place, perched on a stool at the breakfast bar. Zosia and Robert rarely came to see them. It was usually the other way round.

"Have you seen your mother?" Robert asked Janina.

"Don't tell me you've lost her," said Janina, the thought of oncoming domestic tension making her flippant.

"She's disappeared," said Robert.

"Like mother like daughter," Owen said, a trifle testily Janina thought – and in a quasi-quiet tone that ended up sounding louder than the rest of the conversation.

"Accidentally or on purpose?" asked Janina, unable to arrest the flippancy now it had got underway – and especially as Owen seemed annoyed by it.

"It's your mother we're talking about," said Owen, a hint of disapproval in his voice.

Some male bonding between her father and her husband had obviously been going on while she was compromising in the clothes shop. Janina could just imagine the conversation. It would have featured the unpredictability of women's behaviour.

"Well," she said, the imagined conversation helping her warm to her theme, "it could be the successful climax of a trick she's been perfecting for some time. Perhaps we're meant to be applauding."

She noticed the two men were gazing at her with a mixture of incredulity and annoyance.

"My mother's turned seventy," said Janina, as she put away the groceries, banging the cupboard doors more noisily than was necessary. "I'm sure she can look after herself."

"I'm not sure she's in her right mind," said Robert. "She doesn't know what she's doing."

"Granny's gone mad," said Eve, popping her head round the back door cheerfully.

"Craaaazy," said Lidka, joining her sister.

"Don't talk about your grandmother like that," said Owen, glaring at Janina as if the girls taking such a disparaging view of their grandmother's mental stability had been all her doing.

"How do you mean 'she's not in her right mind'?" Janina asked Robert.

"She just packed a couple of bags and disappeared while I was in the garden," he said.

"Did she leave a note saying where she'd gone?" asked Janina, picturing a note in her mother's rather childlike handwriting.

Taking a trip into mental derangement. Your tea's in the oven, Janina imagined it might have said.

"No," said Robert.

"That would suggest she doesn't want to be found then," said Janina.

"She disappeared once before you know," said Robert. "About twenty-five years ago."

Janina had no recollection of her mother disappearing before but, if Robert said she had, she must have done. She felt naive at her own surprise. Her mother and father's relationship had always seemed like a listed building, something planned, built and maintained according to natural or civic laws. Changes to usage would never gain planning permission; would never even be applied for. Feelings and needs were not things that could alter the structure of the building, they merely influenced the decor of the rooms.

All the major domestic arguments between her parents had revolved around food. Her mother had made a dramatic change in culinary direction in the mid-nineties. When Janina was young, they'd had a traditional roast every Sunday. This had always been followed by jelly and ice cream. Zosia had suddenly gone out on a limb and replaced the jelly and ice cream with a biscuit based lemon meringue pie. Robert hadn't reacted well to this change. No doubt he'd considered it flighty behaviour. He'd not been overjoyed either when Zosia had expanded her cooking repertoire from a variety of casserole dishes to such things as lasagne and moussaka, or when she'd insisted on renaming her regular egg and bacon flan 'quiche'.

There'd been another domestic maelstrom when Zosia had gone through what Janina referred to, with well-meant sarcasm, as her 'Caribbean phase'. Zosia had insisted on putting tinned pineapple chunks in everything she made.

"I can't think what I've done wrong to be honest," said Robert.

Janina looked at him. Perhaps Robert hadn't actually done anything wrong. Perhaps he just hadn't done anything particularly right. Perhaps that state of affairs was no longer enough for Zosia. It was a difficult concept to verbalise – especially to her father. However well she managed to express it, he would still have difficulty with the concept. She was saved from any attempt by the sudden eruption of an inappropriately jaunty ringtone from her mobile.

"That will be your mother," said Owen.

It wasn't, it was Bill Gupta.

"Gertie's back, if you still want to talk to her about that Russian translation," he said.

"I'll come over," said Janina.

"Where is she?" asked Owen as soon as Janina put the phone down.

"She's just got back from the airport," said Janina. It was only when she noticed Owen and Robert's stunned expressions that she realised they both still thought it had been her mother on the phone. Because she was annoyed with Owen and Robert's attitude towards her mother, and because she still felt slightly disorientated by the new perception of her parents' relationship, she decided not to re-educate them right away. It was their fault if they jumped too easily to self-involved conclusions.

"She was sent as a delegate to a women's conference in Delhi," added Janina.

"She went to Delhi?" asked Owen incredulously.

"Apparently the smog is much better than it was on her last visit," said Janina.

"She's been before?" asked Robert.

"Every year, it seems," said Janina. She made a quick exit while the two men were still mulling over this surprising news.

25

Janina was aware that if it hadn't been for Robert's alliance with Owen, she would have felt more sympathetic towards her father's predicament. Knowing why she was less sympathetic should have been enough for her to adjust her feelings, but sometimes it takes emotional acceptance a long time to catch up with rational understanding. It was comparable to the difference between the speed of light and the speed of sound – one simply travelled much faster than the other. In terms of her father's plight, Janina could clear the sonic barrier but she couldn't travel back in time.

Comforted by placing her troubling attitude to her father's discomfort within this scientific metaphor, Janina started to feel more concern for him. She hoped, if he needed to use the toilet while he was at their house, he would visit the small downstairs cloakroom. If he went upstairs to the bathroom, he might bump into Gladys. Janina wasn't sure, given his present crisis, how well Robert would cope with meeting his deceased mother reincarnated as a dead spider. Although Gladys was invisible, he might sense her presence and, if she was in Italian mode that day, the pronounced Italian accent certainly wouldn't help. She remembered that Robert wasn't too fond of anything Italian. It was some prejudice passed on to him by an uncle who'd had a nasty experience with an Italian ex-prisoner of war in the late nineteen forties. With this on her mind, Janina made her way to Bill and Gertie Gupta's.

Gertie was Bill's nickname for his younger sister. Her real

name was Jasmine but she'd narrowly escaped being called Gertrude when she was born. When Bill himself had been born, his grandparents, on the English side of the family, had thought it only fair that since he was to have an Indian surname, he should have an English first name. He ended up being called after his grandfather, William. When Gertie was born, her grandmother had, therefore, assumed that Bill's little sister would be named after her. Bill's parents were horrified and started a family row by calling her Jasmine instead. Bill insisted on calling her Gertie Gupta and the name had stuck.

Having met her once, Janina couldn't help thinking that the name Gertie suited her. Everything about Gertie seemed huge, though she wasn't a physically large woman. It was her personality that was expansive. If personalities were measured in bra sizes then Gertie's would have just about squeezed into a 40 DD.

Janina pressed the front door bell to the house that brother and sister now shared.

"Come to analyse what I've got on my washing line today?" asked Bill.

"No, I did that on my last visit," said Janina.

"And?" said Bill.

"It showed that you're an incredible optimist," said Janina.

Bill raised his eyebrows.

"Gertie's in the kitchen with a friend – someone she went to Delhi with," he said. "I'm absolutely sure you're going to love her."

"Ah, the optimism," said Janina.

"I'm never optimistic without reason," said Bill. "And I've every good reason for assuming you'll get on famously with Gertie's new friend."

Janina could find no rational reason why Zosia should be sitting in the home of her failed lover, talking to his sister and eating a large slice of buttered toast with what looked like a generous dollop of strawberry jam. For a moment, Janina wondered whether it was all her own doing – if it was because she'd let Robert and Owen think that Zosia had been to Delhi, that it had actually come true.

"Janina," said Zosia, rather indistinctly because of a mouthful of toast. "I didn't bring back any presents from Delhi because there wasn't time. We went to the conference and had a quick wander round the Chandni Chowk but it was very crowded."

For once, Janina was stunned into silence.

"Women's conference," said Zosia, by way of explanation, as if women's conferences were things she'd been popping off to all her life and were a natural progression from making biscuit based lemon meringue pies instead of jelly. "I don't think your father will have even noticed I'm not at home."

"He has noticed," said Janina. Though she was starting to wonder just when it was that Robert had realised his wife wasn't there. After all, he'd only come round earlier that day and Zosia, it seemed, had managed to travel to and from the Indian sub-continent, attend a conference and saunter round a crowded souk.

"Zosia answered an advert I put in the paper," said Gertie, unable to restrain herself any longer from spilling into the conversation.

Janina looked at her mother for explanation.

"For a sewing and embroidery expert," said Zosia. "Your father won't go anywhere or do anything. He's always messing about in the garden, so I thought I'd do something to keep myself busy."

"It was to help with the Asian women's sewing classes," said Gertie.

Gertie had set up sewing classes for women from a wide range of cultural backgrounds. She applied the term 'sewing' very loosely and couldn't actually sew a stitch herself. She'd always been all fingers and thumbs and never got beyond the threading the needle stage. In the room behind the large poster proclaiming *Sewing Class* in felt tip pen on coloured sugar paper, all sorts of activities had taken place. The label of 'sewing' was a disguise for covert operations. There were English language classes, assertiveness training, computer programming, electrical engineering, art history and self-defence to name just a few.

After the women had been going to the classes for a few months, some of their husbands started to ask them what they were learning.

"Oh, loads of new things," the women told them, and reeled off a list of martial arts stances, past participles, electrical components and various lesser-known art movements which, their husbands, in their limited knowledge, took to be advanced kinds of petit point or broderie anglaise.

"Some of the women decided that they really would like to do a bit of sewing," said Gertie. "That's why I put the advert in the paper."

"It's been great fun," said Zosia. "We made clothes and then lots of embroidered slogans in English and three Asian languages."

"Show Janina the banner we took to Delhi," said Gertie.

Zosia unfurled a large purple banner made from a silky fabric that looked familiar. Gertie held one end and Zosia the other and they stretched it out across the Guptas' kitchen. The banner was beautifully stitched in gold and silver to spell out a message.

SAY 'NO' TO GENDER BASED ROLE DIVISION IN THE HOME.
WE DEMAND EQUALITY FOR ALL WOMEN NOW!
TOMORROW WILL NOT DO!

"Pithy," said Bill.

"We've got versions in Hindi and Urdu," said Zosia. "We're still working on the Punjabi one."

"Blimey, Mum," said Janina with admiration.

She pictured her mother with the women, sewing the seeds of resistance with a cross stitch here and a star stitch there; subverting the course of domestic equilibrium steadily, neatly, with a superior embroidery thread.

Janina had a cup of tea and a slice of toast, and Gertie gave her the Russian poems for translating.

"Shall I tell Dad you're alright then?" Janina asked Zosia, as she left.

"If you like," said Zosia.

Janina was dazed. People set all their living into a small space, within the structure of a limited number of meaningful relationships. Everything outside those structures came to be seen as external. Now, her mother had loosened her moorings, widened the scope of her friendships and set off in a small boat into an ocean of choppy new beginnings.

She visualised Zosia bobbing about on the waves. She was wearing a sou'wester and had a packed lunch – like the ones she'd made for Janina when she was a child. There was a slice of heavily symbolic lemon meringue pie in the Tupperware box along with some fish paste sandwiches and, to Janina's surprise, two lamb samosas and a slightly overcooked vegetable pakora. Zosia had tucked her diary under her arm – her dreams having breached the night time floodgate and invaded her waking life. Janina felt like a child again, unreasonably and ridiculously like a little girl left on the beach as her mother bobbed away, on the outgoing tide.

Janina felt in her pocket for the phone number Alex at the Queen's Head had given her. She took out her mobile and dialled the number.

She wondered why she was going through the motions of answering the advert. Then she thought again about the vulnerability of her hanging space in the wardrobe and about her mother out on the open sea of possibilities, heading off to new horizons. She thought of the smell of bleach that lingered in the kitchen and about Robert, who might also still be lingering, wanting Janina to tell him that Zosia was returning.

"Hello," said a voice at the other end of the phone.

"I'm phoning about the belly dancing," Janina said quickly before she could change her mind and ring off.

"This may sound an odd request from a stranger," said Shaz. "But do you think you could come and meet me at the petrol station? I'm wearing a small primrose coloured towel and a Doc Marten boot."

26

While Shaz was waiting for Janina, she found a car wash token in her bag. She'd bought it the last time she filled the tank but hadn't had time to use it. She decided she might as well make use of it now.

Shaz loved the car wash as much as some people love going to the hairdressers. It was soothing, tranquil – a retreat for a few minutes from the hustle and bustle. She felt a sense of reassurance the second she inserted the token in the slot and manoeuvred the car between the guide rails. She stopped as her front tyres touched the buffer. She pressed the green button, wound the window up and waited expectantly, knowing that in a second, she would hear the water start to spray downwards. Soon she was surrounded by the soft nylon brushes massaging the water and foam – tending, cleaning, polishing. Everything else was suspended. She was encapsulated in the centre of an impersonal, undemanding world.

When Shaz had gone to the car wash once with her boyfriend, he'd seen the interval as an interruption to the busy flow of his day. He said the detergents were too abrasive, that the metal components of the machinery might scratch the car, not to mention the potential dangers to appendages, such as the aerial and wing mirrors.

Perhaps he found Shaz abrasive, like the detergents in the car wash. Maybe he thought that sustained contact with her might scratch his own bodywork and bend his own appendages. But today he wasn't with Shaz in the car wash. Today, he was no longer with her at all.

She'd been oblivious to the world for a few days while she'd been suffering from an unexpected summer flu. When she'd opened her eyes that morning, feeling better, there was a strange hush, as if the house had become hollow.

Everything in the bedroom had disappeared. The wardrobe had gone, the dressing table had gone, the drawers, even her clothes. This included the nightdress she'd been wearing when she first took to her bed. She vaguely remembered discarding it and flinging it to the floor when she was burning up with fever. She stood – naked – in the bedroom, her head still slightly woozy and her legs weak. Next, she discovered that the furniture in the other bedroom had gone too and, downstairs, the television was missing. The sofa, the matching chair, the dining table, the fridge, the washing machine and the contents of the kitchen cupboards, all had disappeared.

Her boyfriend had moved out, taking everything with him while she was too ill to know. He hadn't even left a note of explanation. All that remained in the whole house was one primrose coloured bath towel, one diamante earring for pierced ears, a black Doc Marten boot (size five) and her mobile. Presumably these items had just been an oversight.

When she looked out of the window, she'd been relieved to find that her car was still there. Myrta, the next-door neighbour's cat was sitting on the roof of the little red Fiat washing her face, oblivious to any trauma that the owner of the car might be experiencing.

Shaz found that her handbag was under the bed, where she always hid it in case of intruders. She put on the one Doc Marten boot, the one diamante earring and secured the primrose towel, as demurely as possible, around her body. Tucking her handbag under her arm, she ventured self-consciously to her car. Myrta relinquished it to its owner and jumped onto the roof of the next parked car to finish cleaning behind her ears. The tank of Shaz's car was practically empty. It was only when she reached the petrol station that she fully realised her awkward position. She drew up for a moment in the forecourt and had been plucking up the courage to get out in her strange attire when Janina phoned.

While Shaz was in the car wash, she was transformed into a euphoric state. Lots of new ideas had been chasing round in her mind the last few months, encouraged by a part-time research degree she'd started on gender. Her thinking crystallised under the soapy ministrations of the giant nylon brushes. If she'd scrimped on the token and bought a standard wash or only upgraded to an ordinary super wash, then the transformation might not have happened. The extra three-minute super-hot wax polish may have been responsible. Lack of food, her boyfriend's disappearance, shock at finding an empty house, and a lingering high temperature could also have played a part in her heightened state of consciousness.

It was in this state that Janina found her. They introduced themselves, filled the car up with petrol and then went shopping to get Shaz some clothes – a couple of pairs of trousers, some skirts, sequined tops, a pair of high heels and a faux fur leopard skin jacket. Then, after a quick bite to eat in a café, it was time for Shaz to give her belly dancing lesson. Janina was keen to come along and watch.

27

Shaz's class took place in a large room up a flight of steps at the back of a church. It was made up of a mixture of women, some of Arabic origin, from Morocco, Egypt and Algeria, while others included a Swedish-Estonian jazz singer, a deep-sea diver of Australian origin, a French checkout assistant from Sainsbury's, a handful of wild Turkish students and some pale English women of various shapes and ages.

The scant air of the hall gradually gave way to fiery warmth, the music soaking into it like a rich cognac diffusing through a tumbler of tap water. Janina wondered what brought the women here. Some were, perhaps, homesick for a faraway homeland, while others wanted to keep fit but were bored with aerobics, one or two with the intention of becoming professional dancers or just wanting to enjoy the sense of their own bodies being freed by the music.

"It's too warm to go to the pub this evening," said Shaz, when the class finished. The other women dispersed.

"Let's go for a walk," said Janina. "We could have a wander through the park."

"Let's grab a bottle of wine to take with us," said Shaz.

As they meandered, looking for a good place to sit, Shaz told Janina how she'd grown up in North Africa and had been married off to a North African man who lived in England when she was only sixteen. The marriage hadn't been a success and Shaz had learnt English in order to secure a divorce. She'd got a GCSE as well in the process. Shaz had always had a passion for clothes and cosmetics so she'd enrolled on a beauty therapy course. She'd eventually got a job with a cosmetics company. She'd also gained a second husband, an Englishman – a professional golfer called Clifford.

Shaz met Clifford in a wine bar. She'd developed the habit of flicking peanuts at any man who caught her eye. Clifford did just that. Her first flick propelled a peanut right into the middle of his glass and their eyes met across a vodka-clouded bar. She propelled herself, like a peanut, into a second disastrous relationship. Clifford was charming, good looking and a gambler.

Clifford struggled on the margins of professional golf, making only a modest income, so he stole from Shaz to fund his gambling habit. He also had the disagreeable habit of destroying any letters that arrived from her family and refused to have anything North African in the house.

It was Clifford's objection to her home country that gave Shaz the need to dance. She practised when he was away. As a professional golfer, Clifford was away a lot and she started to do the occasional engagement at a local Turkish restaurant. A diner asked her if she'd teach her how to dance. So Shaz did. Then she set up a class. Clifford found out and forbade it. This time the divorce was much quicker. Shaz didn't need to learn a new language.

"And now I've left the cosmetics company and got a new career," said Shaz. "I'd been leading a perfume campaign but I'd been asking myself a lot of questions about the ethics of advertising."

They walked past the children's playground, the long disused aviaries and the Chinese rock gardens and on, deeper, into the park.

"The new role seemed exactly the right thing at the right time."

"Great," said Janina. "What's the job?"

"Women's equality officer," said Shaz.

"That's quite a change of direction," said Janina.

"It's a good move for me," said Shaz. "The local authority were advertising the post. I applied and was successful."

Janina laughed, looking at Shaz in her sequinned top, short skirt and high heels.

"Is a belly dancer the ideal person?" she asked. "It should be a woman in flat shoes and dungarees or a 'femocrat' with a sharp suit, shouldn't it?"

"What you wear shouldn't have anything to do with it, should it?," said Shaz. "I may have more sequins than the role strictly needs but I've got a degree in Women's Studies and an almost completed research degree. Besides, being a dancer is ideal."

"How's that?" asked Janina.

"The local authority's main function is to choreograph a huge urban dance," said Shaz. "Over the years, the buildings move backwards and forwards, and up and down as some are demolished, others built. Highways are widened or rerouted, the traffic flow ebbs and advances as new roads are built. Directions vary as one-way systems are introduced."

Too engrossed in conversation to find a suitable place to sit, the two women had been wandering along drinking the bottle of chilled Italian wine as they went. They'd passed the long-deserted aviary and the back of the redundant animal enclosure. They hadn't noticed the trees and shrubs around them had thickened. They hadn't even been alarmed by the call of strange birds. They'd paid no attention to the more exotic looking flowers that surged up, striped and vibrant, from the grassy floor and wound with thick creepers up the branches of the tall trees.

Shaz started to dance among the trees that were steadily thickening around them.

"Traffic systems dictate the direction of the dance," she said, expanding on her theme.

"Traffic lights syncopate the rhythm," added Janina.

"The whole dance can reveal the hidden power struggles in the wings," said Shaz. "No one takes women's needs into consideration. That'll be part of my job, to work with the planning and policy units; to make them take notice of our needs. I'm ready to set a new tempo and some new steps."

Shaz took another step herself and tripped over a tree root. "Where are we?" she asked, looking around. "I don't recognise anything. Is that a guava tree over there?"

"And what was that noise?" said Janina with a shiver, despite the heat.

"A fox?" asked Shaz doubtfully, as the evening light, all at once, caramelised from pale lemon to a deep butterscotch. The women looked at each other – now wary.

There was a crashing sound, as if something was forcing its way through the nearby trees, and then – with a flurry of wings – a large green and blue bird burst from the undergrowth, a peach and crimson striped bloom held in its beak. The parrot flapped round in a circle above the women's heads then landed on Shaz's shoulder.

She yelped, trying to brush the bird off. Its wings beat against her hair and she could feel its claws through the thin fabric of her new T-shirt.

Completely unperturbed by Shaz's waving arms, the parrot stopped flapping its wings, settled comfortably on her head and opened its beak – dropping the flower into her hair. Shaz's heartbeat gradually slowed to a less frantic pace.

"An end to oppression and to all fundamentalist beliefs,"

said the parrot, cocking its head to one side and giving Janina a slow wink.

"The wish to overcome oppression must formulate in the minds of the oppressed," it added. Then, as if as an afterthought: "Come on over to my place."

With another flurry of wings, it took off, weaving a bright shot of colour through the urban twilight. It circled back towards them before landing on a tree a little distance away. Janina and Shaz stared at each other for a moment and gave the parrot's speech some thought. Then, because its views on oppression sounded in line with their own, and because they didn't particularly have any alternative plans, they saw no reason why they shouldn't take advantage of its kind invitation.

28

One minute Shaz and Janina were in a park, which had turned into a forest, and the next they were facing a washing line of damp clothes. The laundry hung swathed in mild moonlight. The items weren't suspended in the order of the colours of the rainbow like Bill Gupta's, nor were they scaling the line like fibrous creepers on Warsaw balconies. This washing was on a rotary line, which was in danger of being swamped by sub-tropical foliage. It was situated in what looked as if it had once been the centre of a large suburban lawn; the lawn having gradually shrunk as trees and shrubs had advanced – creeping slowly, like wild arboreal creatures with no concept of trespass grazing on domestic land. In the moonlight, the fabric of Lily's white underwear and blouses had taken on the appearance of softly spun quartz, as if hard silicates had relaxed their grip, loosened out of crystal-line prisms to fluffiness; an acquiescence into yarn. Under the gaze of Janina and Shaz, the sensible knickers became self-conscious; shocked but delighted by the revelation of their own translucence.

Janina and Shaz stared at them transfixed.

"Perhaps we sat down and fell asleep and we're dreaming," said Janina.

She shut her eyes and stumbled forward a little further to see if that would wake her up. But when she cautiously reopened them, she saw an elderly lady reading on a sofa beneath a guava tree. There was a large fringed standard lamp at her side and a cat sitting on her lap.

"I'm so sorry to intrude," said Janina, walking towards her. "We seem to be lost."

Lily raised her head from her book and smiled at them.

"You look as if you could do with a cup of tea," she said.

The woman didn't seem taken aback at all by two people appearing in her dining room.

Shaz and Janina weren't the first unexpected visitors to recently turn up at Lily's home. The house had taken on an energy, which attracted people towards it. A slow flow of visitors, who were probably the interesting people Monica had glimpsed in the tea leaves, had started to arrive.

There were, of course, some normal and rational reasons for people appearing at Lily's house. For instance, the advertisements she'd put in the local paper about her new palm reading skills. Some of Lily's guests arrived conventionally at her front door – as Fatima had. But others turned up unannounced in her dining room – often in the evening – after journeying from some unknown starting point in the forest.

Lily invited Janina and Shaz to sit down. There were two chairs at the other side of the standard lamp. Then she asked whether they would like milk in their tea, edged the cat off her lap and left them to take in their surroundings.

The large black cat disappeared with Lily but was back a few moments later with another cat, a small tortoiseshell, that had two pronounced smudges of black fur above its eyes. Václav Havel and Frida Kahlo sat a short distance from Shaz and Janina, regarding them with knowing blue eyes.

Their eyes reminded Shaz of her neighbour's cat Myrta. She wasn't sure whether she was in a forest or a house or an inexplicable hybrid of the two. There were hybrids of different varieties of flower, of course, but a hybrid between an architectural structure and a large tract of living vegetation was something she'd not come across before.

Lily came back with steaming tea in china cups.

"How rude of me not to introduce myself properly," she said. "I'm Lily and this is Lolita."

She nodded towards the parrot who was now perched on a bookshelf. "How rude," said Lolita and flew out, pointedly, through the trees.

"Are you the same Lily who advertised parrots in the paper?" asked Janina. Because it had been such a surprising day, it didn't seem such an odd coincidence as it might have done on a different day.

"Yes," replied Lily. "And perhaps you two are some of the people who Monica saw in the tea leaves." She didn't go on to explain what she meant by that or who Monica might be.

Shaz and Janina introduced themselves and because Lily seemed interested and in no hurry to do anything other than listen to their life stories, they told them. The cats prowled around the room and Lolita fluttered in and out, perching on different items of furniture before taking off into the moonlit forest again.

Shaz was just about to tell Lily about her research work on Images of the Female Gender as Presented Through Twenty-First Century Transvestism when they were interrupted by shouting.

"There are some amnesiacs in my living room," said Lily. "I'd forgotten all about them. They're watching *Desperately Seeking Susan*."

29

The job of mowing the lawn couldn't be put off any longer. When Fatima mentioned this to Salah, he didn't show any interest whatsoever. She decided she'd have to squeeze the job into her own never-ending list of things to do. As a reward to herself, she'd cook an especially nice meal that evening and go over to see Lily afterwards. She'd not been to Lily's for a couple of weeks. Fatima got out the lawn mower and cut the grass, methodically, logically. She followed a track from one side of the house to the other and back. She repeated this sequence until she'd covered the length of the lawn in her zigzag progress, she and the lawn mower side-winding like one entity, half woman, half electrically-powered garden appliance. When she'd finished, she sat down with a glass of lemonade underneath the shade of the plum tree. She stared up at the leafy branches, thankful for a rest after her exertion in the sun. After the picnic in Lily's forest, Lily had lent Fatima more books on politics and philosophy and Fatima had been to the library to get some on trees. It was an area of botanical knowledge that she'd previously shied away from because of her fear of forests.

Leaning against the tree, she closed her eyes, shutting out the rest of the world. She thought about the pulse of sap pumping through the green veins, how it spun its yearly rings as it crept towards the sky. Each cross-section of the tree trunk was the story of its existence, preserved in living tissue. With each fresh year, its chloroplast-filled fingertips reached out for light. Fatima wished her life was more like that of a tree. She'd lost a sense of growth, of secret green unfolding into cool air.

She would have been happy to stay contemplating under the plum tree for longer but there were other things to do. She trimmed the edges of the lawn with the strimmer and then went indoors. She wanted to talk about trees, about life, to Salah but he was watching a late afternoon film on one of the movie channels. It was some involved psychological thriller set in a future world and, unable to pick up the plot at such a late stage, Fatima went out shopping. Her plan was to buy ingredients for the extra-special evening meal she'd promised herself.

Between leaving her house and arriving at the nearest supermarket, she decided that the meal was to be the story of her life, delivered through the colours and flavours of food. She would choose the ingredients carefully to symbolise the elements of her experiences so far – her memories, her feelings. She was egged on by Violet, who strolled along with her and who (not surprisingly, given her own adventurous approach to cooking) seemed to approve of the project. Fatima wasn't sure where the idea had come from. Maybe, late one night, while waiting for the fast colour cycle on the washing machine to finish, she'd caught part of an avant-garde film with subtitles, which had suggested that cooking could be a form of autobiographical expression.

She bumped into a neighbour at the entrance to the shop and trotted out the expected questions about the health and weight of her newly born nephew. But her interest was elsewhere, reaching out to fulfil her culinary creation. She could hardly wait to get her hands on the ingredients she needed. There was something more now to the goods on the shelves. There was more than the promise of special offers, more than the informative and concise table of contents detailing the number of calories coiled within each packet. The supermarket shelves had become vats brimming with different coloured 'paint' and Fatima wanted to leap in, like some experimental artist, rolling herself around on the splayed blank canvas of the shop floor.

It was when she started exploring the shelves that her enthusiasm began to falter. The limited imagination of the store manager set her an insurmountable problem. It was going to be hard translating the meaning of her life into a recipe based on any of the items in the shop. Her eyes took in the cans of pilchards, rice, noodles, corned beef, stewing steak, milk, breakfast cereal and fruit juice, sugar, yoghurts, cauliflower, lettuce and potatoes. She decided, reluctantly, that her plan had been over-ambitious.

If she'd derived the idea subconsciously from a film, it had probably been French. French shops, no doubt, were stocked with more promising raw materials. There would be cheeses with pungent centres oozing yellow promises through their thick rind. There would be fungi plucked from somewhere dark and dank, terrines made from gape-eyed aquatic creatures, and stocks still bearing the odd stripped white bone.

Fatima stared hopelessly into the freezers at the fishcakes and fish fingers – cod, haddock, salmon, crumbed and battered. A larger supermarket might have had more potential but, since there was no large store on her side of town, her project would have to be put on ice. Instead, Fatima bought the ingredients for a spaghetti Bolognese and splashed out on a deluxe tub of ice cream to have with strawberries.

After the meal, she sat beneath the plum tree again. If she couldn't relate her own life story through flavour, she'd write it down. She wrote for two hours and, at the end of that time, decided to send her creation to her cousin in Morocco. She was a storyteller by trade and she could read it out for all to hear in the market square of her home town. Fatima scribbled a quick note and then put it all in an envelope. She knew that no one would fight wars over the meaning of the story. No one would pronounce fatwas against her. No one would discuss whether the narrative was meant to be taken literally or symbolically. But perhaps someone – maybe many someones – would hear it and understand it.

"Aah," they would say and nod. And the *aah* would be like the sound of new green life greeting the buoyancy of air.

Salah was watching the news as Fatima stood in the living room doorway. She opened her mouth to tell him where she was going but different words came out.

"What would it be like to be a tree?" she found she'd said.

The words hung in the air for a moment, as if she'd stepped into the avant-garde film and her intended sentence had been translated incorrectly. Violet, who'd been cleaning behind her ears, froze with her paw in mid-air. She gave her head a little incredulous shake at Fatima. They both held their breath and waited for Salah's response. He only half looked up.

"Yes, please," he said, "Don't forget to give the sugar a good stir."

"Come in, come in," urged Lily when Fatima knocked on the front door. "I've got some new friends I want you to meet."

Lily took Fatima to the living room. From outside, it sounded as if a party was in full swing. Lily opened the door to reveal two men and two women. A film was just finishing, the credits rolling down the screen while everyone shouted and cheered.

"One struggle, one fight. Amnesiacs of the world …" chanted one of the men.

"What was it we were going to do?" he asked the other with mock concern.

"I can't remember," the man shouted back.

"Unite," said one of the women, who was dressed in a very short skirt, high heels and a sequined T-shirt. "You were going to unite!" She got up and started dancing and singing along to the film's theme tune, Madonna's "Into the Groove", while the others clapped along.

30

Lily tried to do a general round of introductions. This was a more difficult task than it might sound, firstly, because of all the noise and, secondly, because Lily had no idea what either of the men were called. To compound the problem, neither did the men.

After jumping from the back of a privatised ambulance, both of these guests had been drawn to Lily's house by her advert for palm readings. They didn't want to know what was going to happen to them in the future but what had already happened to them in the past. Lily and the amnesiacs were, in a way, reverse representations of each other. The men, due to the unnerving speed of the ambulance service, had lost their memories and were searching for their old lives. Lily, as a result of the slow arrival of the same service and her husband's subsequent demise, had regained her previous aspirations and started a new life.

Lily invited everyone back into the dining room, insisting that they must all have something to eat. Janina and Shaz told Fatima how they'd wandered through the park and come across Lolita and how, after Lolita flew off, they'd stumbled on through the ever-thickening trees and flowers.

Everyone got to know each other while they ate stuffed wild mushrooms and breadfruit and coconut soup. Then they moved on to lamb, sautéed in a rich Madeira sauce, accompanied by dishes of creamed and glazed sub-tropical vegetables.

Lily had made guava and honey tartlets with chocolate marshmallow sauce for dessert, plus a pudding of her own creation, concocted from exotic fruits and the three remaining cans of Ernest's tapioca pudding. These cans had been at the back of a cupboard and so had missed being despatched to the local homeless.

While they ate, everyone exchanged stories – except the amnesiacs who just listened. The night advanced, moonlight slanting through the gaps in the heavily foliaged garden. Lily brought out a homemade rum punch and Václav and Frida Kahlo, accompanied by Lolita, roosted in the bonsai tree which, due to the influence of the rum, now seemed to sway slightly in the tropical breeze.

"Biographies of people who have no past, that would be a real challenge," said Fatima.

The amnesia sufferers decided, however, that loss of memory provided no serious deterrent to reliving the past and started to make up exciting scenarios from previous lives. One of them claimed they'd spent five years herding reindeer with the Sami people of the Arctic regions of Finland and another said he'd been involved in espionage but was prevented from revealing any details due to strict secrecy protocols.

Shaz began to tell everyone what she'd been thinking about while she was in the car wash. Later, Fatima tried to write down what Shaz had said but it was almost impossible because the manner in which Shaz presented her thoughts became part of the message itself. Her main idea was that there was too much negativity in the world. If people avoided all the negative clutter, they would start to feel the spin of the Earth, the fluidity of matter. They would come to appreciate how everything was constantly changing yet always connected; that perceptions are dulled to fit with a far too narrow a view of reality. Shaz had started to draw and dance and sing as she explained, and the others didn't need much encouragement to join in. It was like an audience participation drama but much, much wilder.

At the end of the performance everyone broke into applause and Shaz, exhausted, started to yawn.

"You must stay here," Lily said to her. "Would you like me to make up the spare bed or would you prefer a hammock slung from the guava trees?"

Shaz opted for the hammock and everyone else started to make their way home, except the amnesiacs who didn't know where home was and had set up a camp of improvised yurts in the forest. They all promised to meet at Lily's again soon.

It was odd, thought Janina as she walked home, but she could distinctly feel the spin of the Earth now that Shaz had mentioned it. She stopped for a moment under a lamp post to feel the full effect. She wondered why she'd never felt it before. Carlotta eyed her suspiciously from under the cover of a nearby hedge as Janina swayed, very slightly, before walking the last few metres towards her front gate.

"Where've you been?" asked Owen as Janina got into bed, only a couple of hours before Owen's alarm clock was due to wake him for another full day of safety checks and risk assessments. "Did you talk some sense into your mother?"

"It wasn't necessary," said Janina. "She is fully in charge of her own mental faculties." Janina was still experiencing the spinning of the planet. She didn't seem to be able to stop the sensation now that she'd become aware of it. She also felt an uncharacteristic need to communicate with Owen – to share with him some of her experiences from the last few hours.

"I went to buy petrol for a woman wearing a primrose coloured towel. She's a belly dancing equalities officer. Then a parrot found us and invited us to a picnic with a palm reader called Lily. We ate in her tropical forest. There were lots of interesting people. There were two men who didn't know who they were and a biography-writing florist," said Janina. "There were bonsai trees that were seven feet tall. Václav Havel and Frida Kahlo were sitting in a nest at the top."

Owen was silent.

"Lily's husband died after an ancient goddess arranged a nasty accident with a milk bottle," added Janina after a few moments.

Owen sighed.

31

Janina was soon fast asleep, despite the stifling stratosphere that lay across the city like a high tog duvet, making the streets swelter. She slipped into the dream where Owen was Lenin and she was Alexandra again. This dream started where the other one left off – with Alexandra reminding Lenin that he was supposed to be an advocate of Leninism.

"If I was all for it in 1918," said Lenin. "There's no reason why I shouldn't change my views over a period of more than a hundred years."

"There is if you've been dead for most of them," said Alexandra.

"I might have had a change of heart in the afterlife," said Lenin, sulkily.

"There is no afterlife, remember?" said Alexandra. "I do believe you've renounced historical materialism and become an idealist."

"And I believe," retorted Lenin, with a triumphant glint in his eye. "That if I've been dead for the last century, then you have become a necrophiliac."

Alexandra's annoyance woke Janina up again. Owen was already awake. He had to go to work, even though it was Saturday, to cover for colleagues on summer holidays. He'd had a restless night waiting for Janina to return home. When she finally appeared, the conversation he'd had with her had done little to ease him into a trouble-free sleep. He was getting dressed on the edge of the bed when Janina awoke from the dream and half sat up.

"I'm not a necrophiliac," she said to Owen, before laying down and going straight back to sleep. Owen tried to think of a suitable reply as he tucked his tie into his trousers, but he couldn't. He turned the fan on to high, went downstairs and had a bowl of cornflakes instead.

Tuned into any sounds of life coming from his own home, Gus, the cat, could hear Owen clinking dishes all the way from the other end of the street. He abandoned his attempts to impress Fatima's cat, Violet, and, slick as melting butter on overdone toast, he slid home; an insignificant detail in the morning street, soon absorbed into the slightly burnt texture of the day. He overtook Carlotta, who was sauntering at a more sedate pace. Violet followed him with her eyes but her paws remained on the kitchen windowsill in the shade of an old quince tree.

Perhaps it was because Janina's head was still spinning a little that, as she dropped back into deeper sleep, she dreamt she was dancing from one season to another on the rim of the turning planet. She stood for a moment, poised on a wet and windy day in October. The day was balanced on the cusp of autumn and winter. If it had been a drawing it would have been executed in charcoal, for the hours of night were smudged, almost imperceptibly, into day.

As Janina leapt confidently to December, she realised that she could diagrammatically represent all the most important events of her life by pinpointing where they happened on the spin trajectory of the Earth. She could have plotted them out on paper in relation to geometric dissections. Everything she'd done could be marked within the diameters of darkness and light, day and night, and within the seasonal quarters – the piercing radii of cold and heat – spring, summer, autumn, winter.

On the December day where she landed, the temperature had fallen. It was no longer wet but dry. The next day there might be snow, for a blue-eyed cat was getting skittish under a bleached sky.

32

Outside Janina's house, the day was placed firmly within the diameter of light and just past midpoint in the seasonal quarter of heat. The queue for breakfast on the back windowsill of Fatima's Blossom Tree had regrouped into a small but vocal demonstration for feline rights. At the other end of the street, Gus and Carlotta were content indoors. Their stomachs were full, the shadows thrown by the slatted blinds transforming them into small tigers lazily sniffing freedom in the air as it squeezed, rectangular, around the edges of the kitchen door.

In her home at the other side of the park, Lily – not inclined to torpor – had been up for hours, clearing discarded glasses and hoovering the forest floor. She knew she must make another attempt to read the amnesia sufferers' palms. She saw virtually nothing when she tried the first time, as if losing their memories had made their pasts less definable, less real and, as a result, the lines that represented them on their palms less pronounced.

She tiptoed around the hammock slung between the guava trees, where Shaz still slept. Then she decided to have a cup of tea and check if there was any post.

Václav Havel was sitting on the doormat, a flyer for a new pizza place lying next to him and a postcard sticking out from under his feet. After unceremoniously grabbing the postcard from beneath him, Lily could see that it bore a view of a windswept winter promenade. She made herself wait until she sat down with her cup of tea before she turned it over. There wasn't a great deal written on it but what was there was intriguing.

"I chose this scene as I know how much you love the seaside in winter," the message began, in almost illegible handwriting. "Thank you for your kind letter to my grandmother, Marlene. Since seeing the letter, I've had some strange tea cup readings about you. Ring me." It was simply signed *Monica Moule*, with a phone number below.

Lily was puzzled for several reasons. Firstly, she had no idea that Monica knew her address, secondly, she had no idea how Monica knew that she preferred the seaside in winter, and thirdly, she had no idea that Monica's surname was Moule. All three of these surprises were explained by the fourth – that Monica was Marlene's granddaughter. It was the first she'd heard of Marlene Moule and Monica being related at all.

She sipped her tea and looked at her post, as if trying to work out how so many surprises could be contained on one small piece of card. Then she went to make another pot of tea and some toast, which she put on a tray along with homemade raspberry and mango preserve. Shaz had woken up and one of the amnesiacs had just arrived, so they carried out a picnic table and it was soon set up beneath the fringe of trees.

Sometimes Monica Moule didn't hear her landline ringing. Griselda had taken to wrapping herself around it to sleep. Luckily, when Lily phoned, the cat was outside sunning herself. When Lily asked Monica if she would help with some palm readings, she didn't take much persuading. Business had been slack recently. Everyone was too busy enjoying the present heat wave to be too concerned about what was going to happen in the future. Customers experiencing memory loss would be a new challenge. It was arranged that she would stay with Lily for a short while.

"How many sugars?" Lily asked one of the amnesia sufferers, after the tea had brewed. But, of course, he didn't know.

He decided to try one spoon. He'd been drinking his tea with no sugar but it hadn't seemed quite right. The other amnesiac (who so far had been drinking his tea with one sugar and thinking much the same thing) decided to try it with two. Both were happy with the new amounts they'd chosen. Lily suggested that the number of spoons of sugar they preferred could become their temporary names: One Spoon and Two Spoons.

Both One Spoon and Two Spoons thought this was a good idea. They'd previously resisted the idea of having new names as it seemed like an acceptance that they'd never reclaim their old identities. But the names One Spoon and Two Spoons were based on recovering knowledge about themselves.

Lily's number of visitors swelled throughout the day. Shaz turned up later in the morning and Fatima, having closed the flower shop at lunchtime, arrived in the afternoon. Owen finished work early and took the girls to the local climbing wall so, after Janina had phoned Robert to tell him that Zosia was safe (but not yet ready to come home), she was also irresistibly drawn back to Lily's. This time she took Gladys with her.

It was when they were all gathered together that Lily mentioned a plan she'd been formulating all day. She'd decided it was time to extend her actions beyond liberating plants. It was time to branch out into human society.

33

Owen was thinking about necrophiliacs. It wasn't a subject that he'd given any thought to before. He wondered why on earth Janina should think he'd ever accused her of being such a thing. He tried to recall recent conversations and how they might have been misinterpreted. All he could remember offhand were some discussions involving putting out the recycling bin and whose turn it was to unload the dishwasher. Neither of these exchanges seemed fertile ground for such a gross misunderstanding.

Owen left the girls with Robert to keep their grandfather company. As Owen was leaving, Robert had been nervously watching his granddaughters playing a game in which Eve pretended to be Zosia and was swept off by a vulture-shaped drone to a newly discovered island just off the coast of Blackpool.

Owen had hovered by the gate for a few seconds wondering whether leaving them with Robert was such a good idea, but he had his own problems he needed to mull over. He didn't think that the subject of these problems was a suitable matter for discussion with his father-in-law.

It was early evening when Owen walked into the Queen's Head. It was almost empty. Alex was having a conversation with Bill Gupta. Bill's relationship with Alex was typical of lots of relationships between bar staff and regular customers. They'd spent quite a few hours in each other's company. If either of them had totted up the amount of time, they would have been surprised. They'd also discussed a wide range of subjects, if only at a superficial level, but there were still a lot of things they didn't know about each other. Their friendship unfortunately substantiated Bill's dream – it would have fitted well into a haberdashery department of human relationships. It would never go beyond bias binding and Velcro.

Because Bill and Alex's relationship lacked a lot of the day to day minutiae, which many conversations depend upon to build up steam, they'd subconsciously established some set pieces. These were subjects which got their conversational strolling underway. They included the price of beer, the wide variety of sausages now available and the advantages and disadvantages of having a monarchy. When Owen came into the bar they'd been meandering around the subject of crocodiles, which for some reason, since Alex had introduced the subject into their conversation, had become one of the starting points for their verbal excursions. Today, it was still in the early stages of development and neither of them were yet sure where it was going.

"Some people think alligators and crocodiles are the same," said Alex.

"Well, they're both reptiles and cold blooded," said Bill.

"One or both were around in prehistoric times," said Alex.

"Yet now some have become endangered species," said Bill. He seemed to remember reading something about it in a book that his ex, Jenny, had on her bookshelves above the aquarium in her flat.

"All the same, if there was a nuclear bomb," said Alex, passing Owen a pint and a packet of dry roasted peanuts. "Crocodiles would be the only things to survive."

"No, that's not right," contested Bill. "It would be ants, not crocodiles."

Owen opened his packet of peanuts. Bill and Alex looked at him expectantly, hoping he might act as adjudicator. But Owen, who usually preferred to keep his personal problems to himself, was desperate to talk to someone about them. He wondered how he could nudge the subject under discussion imperceptibly in that direction.

"Do you think they practice necrophilia?" he blurted out, missing his footing on the slippery surface of subtlety and lurching straight into unknown waters.

There was a pause. They all took a sip of their respective drinks.

"Crocodiles or ants?" queried Bill, after a significant amount of time had elapsed.

"Either," said Owen.

Bill and Alex gave the question considerable thought. Neither was able to give a definitive answer.

Owen's question was doomed to become one of those unanswered mysteries with which life is scattered like, for instance, the whereabouts of Janina's friend's husband who'd disappeared in the supermarket never to be seen again. Janina happened to be recounting this very conundrum to her new friends at the exact moment that Owen was raising his query with Bill and Alex. She was explaining to her listeners that her friend had been in a strange situation. As far as she knew, her partner would never appear in her life again but that knowledge didn't have the final certainty that a medically confirmed death certificate afforded.

In an attempt to fill this void, Janina's friend had concocted what might have been described as a reconstituted husband. She used an elaborate mixture of coat hangers, various items of his clothing, and clothes pegs. At first, she'd worked with the intention of creating an uncanny likeness to the real man but, due to the lack of available materials, the project quickly became an art therapy sculpture of a more impressionistic kind. Once it was finished, she was not sure what to do with it. She left it in the kitchen – leaning aimlessly against the side of the fridge. Soon bits started to drop off and Owen, popping round to pick up Janina, pointed out that it was a health and safety hazard. After that, she moved it into the garden where it eventually became half-heartedly adopted as an unusual trellis for a stray clematis.

One Spoon and Two Spoons wondered whether someone somewhere was missing them. Crickets chirped from the forest undergrowth and, from further away, a peacock shrieked in the resonant evening heat. Warmth, stored from the day, emanated from the ground as the sun started to sink in the sky.

Whether anyone was missing them or not, Shaz was relieved that the memory loss survivors now had names. With her equalities hat on, it had felt inappropriate to be grouping them together, as if they weren't individuals, and seeing their disability rather than the person. She was hoping to follow their fortunes to see how they progressed.

"Things never disappear completely, they're just transformed." said Janina. "Things change into something else."

Janina was thinking about the shrunken jumper. It had been damaged and yet the metamorphosis had given it something additional, something quite extraordinary, at the same time. She thought for a moment that she saw a small crocodile emerge from the bushes, but then it was replaced simply by air again. It was too dark to be sure whether there was anything there or not because of the woven layers of foliage above. The sun had slipped further down the sky. Lolita was perched on One Spoon's shoulder and, aided by fruit punch – the recipe of which required a liberal amount of rum – everyone was in an expansive mood.

Lily decided that now was the time to introduce her idea of benign actions.

"Of course," she said, "there are different kinds of disappearance. People can be made to disappear."

She left a meaningful pause and then explained her plan, which was to capture or – as Lily put it – *invite* selected guests to her house, where they'd be offered new ways of viewing the world. She hoped that after their stay they would go back into the world less harmful to others and happier in themselves.

"All in favour of the plan, raise your glasses," said One Spoon, looking like a pirate with Lolita perching on the top of his head.

Everyone raised their glasses. Shaz celebrated the occasion with a dance. Fatima cheered, even though partially distracted by the thought that Violet might be cooking the tea again in her absence. Only Václav Havel, roosting in the cat-nest at the top of the swaying bonsai tree, exchanged a doubtful glance with Frida Kahlo. But as neither Václav Havel nor Frida Kahlo had a glass to raise, their actions were not noticed or recorded as abstentions.

34

As Monica Moule was stepping off the train from the seaside and onto the platform of the busy city railway station, Lily was stepping out of the bank. She'd popped in to change the name under which she held her account. She'd decided to revert back to her maiden name of Sanderson.

Owen was on his way to work. There were no troubling unknowns in his schedule for the morning, only thoughts of Janina provided unsettling rumble strips as he tried to speed down the one-way system of another day.

Janina, with no work appointments until the afternoon, dropped off the girls at school before going to see if her mother was still a house guest at Bill and Gertie Gupta's.

Zosia was sitting in a deck chair in the Guptas' garden at the far side of the water butt, wearing a pair of red slippers and sewing a large tapestry for all she was worth. Janina presumed it was the Punjabi version of the banners she'd already seen. She approached her mother a little nervously; her mother's recent behaviour making her almost a stranger. The only visible difference Janina immediately noticed was her nails, which she'd painted a rather sophist-icated midnight blue.

"Helix aspersa," said Zosia. She'd transferred her attentions from her sewing to a large brown snail that was transcribing a broken silvery trail across a plank of wood at the side of the flower border. "They're miraculous things, snails."

This one, thought Janina, wasn't anything like as beautiful as the ones on her father's apple trees.

"People think of snails as pests," said Zosia. "But they eat mainly decomposing vegetation. Mind you, they won't say no to the odd fresh leaf."

Janina tended to forget that her mother had been a biologist before she'd given it up to be a full-time mum. She watched a variety of winged insects circling and diving towards the surface of filmy liquid in the water butt.

"He'd have made such a big fuss," said Zosia, as Janina leaned against the washing line post. Janina formed a question with her eyebrows.

"Your father," said Zosia. "About me going to Delhi to the women's conference. That's why I didn't tell him."

"I don't see why," said Janina.

Zosia gave Janina an impatient look, transferring the annoyance she felt towards Robert to Janina, his closest blood relative.

"The flying," she said.

Before retiring, Robert had worked in the aircraft industry. Maybe it was an incidence of familiarity breeding contempt, but having been involved in making planes, he refused to believe in their ability to fly. He thought about the weight of the metal. He thought about the frailty of their structure hanging thousands of feet up in the air, vulnerable man-made instruments ready to succumb to gravity and to the creaking blue weight of ice-cold air. His own feet remained fixed to the surface of the planet; rooted to the earth.

"Promise me you'll never fly," he'd said to Janina when she was small, but she'd never promised. As she'd grown older, he had been forced to acquiesce to her independence. Janina could see how it might be easier for Robert to exert pressure on his wife.

"You just disappeared," said Janina, as she watched a dragonfly skid perfectly onto the filmy landing strip in the water butt.

"It was the only option," said Zosia.

Janina didn't argue. She could see that in the world her parents inhabited – the partially enclosed reality system from which they both viewed outside life – this might be absolutely correct. It wasn't for Janina to decide otherwise.

"The Florida lysiloma tree snail travelled all the way from Cuba on trees felled by a tropical hurricane," said Zosia. "But even under their own steam, snails can travel an amazingly long way in a very short time. People remove them and before they know it, they're back again. It would be an interesting project to mark them in some way and keep track of their individual journeys."

She gave Janina a knowing smile that Janina was at a loss to interpret.

Monica's arrival at Lily's house seemed to set a new pace for Lily's plans. Monica was entranced by Lily's forest and the ideas that had been hatched in the rum-tinged air beneath the moonlit canopy. Lily and Monica consulted astrological charts to find the best date on which to carry out the first action. They worked together to see what they could discern from the palms of One Spoon and Two Spoons. Unfortunately, Monica was able to see little more than Lily had. A third amnesia sufferer appeared at Lily's house the day after Monica arrived. He was immediately invited by the others to stay in the yurts until his memory returned. Lily gave him several cups of tea with varying amounts of sugar, after which he was known as No Spoons.

The others dropped in to see how things were progressing when they could. But they were all busy. Janina had some interpreting to do and Fatima had her flower shop to run. It wasn't until the weekend that they were all back together again.

Everyone still supported direct action. The only disagreement came as a result of trying to decide who they should choose as their lucky first candidate. Some of the nominees were people of national or international infamy. Lily said they'd have to discount these prospective candidates because capturing them would be impossible due to high levels of security or because, in some cases, their nominators – in their enthusiasm to suggest them – had forgotten they were actually dead. They decided to treat the first attempt as a modest pilot and work their way up to bigger fish.

The remaining suggestions were people who the women had their own personal reasons to nominate. Of course, each woman felt that her suggested candidate was better qualified for gaining entry onto the course than those of their fellow conspirators. So, they decided that the successful nominee should be drawn from a hat. To add suitable ceremony to the occasion, Lily brought down an oversized top hat from the loft. She thought it belonged to an ancestor as a label inside bore the name 'Eli Sanderson'. She dusted it off and the women popped in their nomination slips. Lolita was invited to draw one out with her beak. This might have been a good idea if, after picking out a name, Lolita hadn't flown to the top of the bonsai tree and, from there, out into the depths of the tropical woodland. By a process of elimination – using the slips left in the hat – it was eventually revealed that the first student to enter their select academy was to be Shaz's nominee: Jaffa Troy. Jaffa Troy was the deputy director of planning for the local authority. Shaz had come across him in several meetings. He'd stared lecherously at her, making her feel vulnerable. Then after she'd shared a number of innovative new ideas with him, he'd blatantly stolen them and presented them as his own in a report to committee. She had the distinct feeling that he was a kerb crawler of the female intellect.

"What do you do?" he'd ask, winding down the car window and leering at an attractive woman's Double First in Thermal Kinetics.

"Calculus, Latin and Theoretical Physics. Extra for Jungian Psychology and Biochemistry," the answer might be.

The lucky man was totally unaware that he was about to receive a free service that he'd never dreamt of even in his wildest fantasies.

35

Jaffa Troy, the deputy director of planning, was tossing and turning in bed half awake and half asleep. He was wondering about the sanity of modern life and trying to cling on to a few common sense absolutes in the ever-changing world of performance targets and restructuring. Where were new directions in internal quasi-markets and contracting out of services going to end?

Mona Troy, the deputy director of planning's wife, was a great believer in the rejuvenating qualities of a good night's sleep so she was becoming irritated by Jaffa's restlessness. It was preventing her from getting her beauty sleep. She was attempting to calculate how many frown lines might be added to the area around the eyes for each hour of wakefulness. She got up and did some dusting. Mona's mother maintained that her daughter displayed an exemplary attention to household chores. One or two of her friends would have described her cleaning habit less favourably – as bordering on the obsessive.

She was the sort of woman who might have been tempted to spruce up her birth canal with a Brillo pad had she thought of it, but, luckily, she hadn't. She gave the oven and hob an extra polish and dusted the staircase, hoping that Jaffa might have dropped off by the time she got back to bed. He hadn't. It was then that she thought about sex. Not that she was feeling amorous; it just might lull him off.

Oral sex would probably be the quickest option. She'd just squirmed down the bed when she remembered she had to go to her Calories Club that evening. The meeting consisted of a weigh-in and a declaration of the number of calories consumed within the week. The club secretary examined the daily logbook of calorie intake studiously, noting every morsel that had passed each woman's lips. Nothing missed her attention. A stickler for detail, and for abiding by the rules, it didn't occur to Mona that she could omit to declare these contraband calories. She paused. How embarrassing would it be written for all to see in the logbook, and how many calories would it be worth?

Mona edged back up the bed and went downstairs in search of an alternative method of lulling Jaffa off to sleep. Ideally, one that would increase his calorie intake for the day rather than her own. She returned to the bedroom a few minutes later with a steaming mug of Horlicks.

So far, everything had gone to plan. Shaz had secretly accessed Jaffa's personnel file to discover his star sign, and Lily and Monica had consulted astrological charts to identify the most auspicious day for the learning opportunity to start. Shaz had been given the responsibility of luring him out of City Hall via the porter's exit into a yard behind the rubbish skips. The others would be waiting with a large tea cosy in the shape of a Christmas pudding, a car and reassuring words.

Caught up in the excitement of the bigger picture, Shaz hadn't contemplated exactly how she'd lure Jaffa out of the meeting until she was already in it. She nervously slung off her leopard print jacket as she felt panic rising. Then she remembered the peanut flicking technique she'd previously perfected in pubs to attract the attention of men who caught her eye. But City Hall's Committee Room 3 was completely devoid of peanuts.

Shaz searched surreptitiously in her handbag for an alternative and found a bag of unsalted cashews, opened and half-consumed. While everyone was skim reading the abstract of the first report, Shaz plucked up the courage to flick a nut in the direction of the deputy director of planning. It skimmed past the director of traffic and transport's head, narrowly missed the Labour group leader's arm, continued past its intended target and landed with a splash in the chief executive's cup of tea. The real target continued to stare into space without blinking. Shaz threw a handful of cashews into her mouth to aid her thought processes and started to chew.

"What are the main equalities issues we need to be aware of?" asked the chief executive, returning to the first page of the report while looking at Shaz and wiping a spot of tepid tea from the back of his left hand. Shaz had been so lost in thought she had no idea what the chief executive was asking her. She took a deep breath to make an informed sounding but evasive noise and nearly choked on a tiny fragment of semi-chewed nut. She stood up spluttering and, with her eyes streaming, made for the door. The deputy director of planning shook himself from his trance and leapt up to open it for her. He followed her solicitously, trying to be helpful by giving her an occasional pat on the back and asking if she'd like some water. Inwardly celebrating the unplanned, but fortunate, turn of events, she made her way to the porter's entrance.

Doubled over with coughing, she tried to make sure he continued to follow her by giving him a beguiling wink, but her eyes were still watering too much.

"I speak Arabic and learnt the English language fluently in only three months," she tried to whisper seductively, but she was coughing too much for her words to be intelligible. She spluttered round the side of the building towards the skips with the concerned deputy director hot on her heels, still asking if he could be of assistance and waving a wad of tissues at her.

Lily felt a little quirk of conscience as she pulled the woolly tea cosy over his head – ensuring it obscured his vision – and then tied his hands gently behind his back with colourful double ply. The victim, or recipient as Lily preferred to think of him, didn't put up any struggle at all – he was taken too much by surprise. Lily hoped Jaffa's head wouldn't stretch her favourite tea cosy too much. It had been the first suitable item she'd come across in the drawer the previous evening while searching for something to cover the lucky recipient's eyes. As Jaffa was bundled into Shaz's car (it was spotlessly clean and beautifully polished, as Shaz had put it through the car wash for the occasion) for the short journey to Lily's house, Lily repeatedly asked, in a concerned way, if he was alright. It reminded him, for some reason, of the way his grandmother used to repeatedly ask if he was warm enough when he was playing out as a child. He'd found it irritating at the time but now found it quite reassuring and consoling.

Jaffa was quiet during the car ride. He couldn't understand why anyone would want to kidnap him. He tried to work out a logical explanation for his situation. He didn't want to succumb to melodrama when there must be a sensible explanation for him being bundled into a small Fiat with a tea cosy over his head and his hands tied behind his back. He'd once got up for work and found everywhere deserted and had wondered, for a couple of minutes, whether he was the sole survivor of a nuclear attack. But then he'd remembered that it was a bank holiday. Occasionally, he'd turn up to an important meeting to find the venue in ghostly silence only to discover later that the date of the meeting had been changed via an email that he'd forgotten to open. But his current situation was more difficult to explain away with a bank holiday or an item of unread electronic correspondence.

"Let me introduce you to everyone," said Lily, when they reached her house. She manoeuvred their student into an armchair in the dining room and finally removed the tea cosy from his head. Jaffa blinked at the small gathering around him.

"These," said Lily, "are some people who live in a yurt in my forest. I can't introduce them properly as they've forgotten who they are." She smiled apologetically before continuing. "This is Václav Havel, who metamorphosed into a cat, and this is his friend Frida Kahlo. Here's Janina and in her pocket is Gladys, an invisible dead spider."

The prisoner gave up all hope of his safe return to the outside world and wished he still had the woolly Christmas pudding over his head, even though it had been a bit tickly.

"You're the lucky first recipient of our education opportunity, thanks to Shaz," said Lily. "You'll leave this house a happier individual and less of a threat to society."

"I'm not a threat to society," said Jaffa, shrinking back in the armchair.

"That's what they all say," said Shaz. "I bet you sneak out of people's lives when they've got flu and take all their belongings with you."

"And forget to pick up your daughters from school," said Janina.

"I imagine it's never occurred to you to do some of the cooking and cleaning," accused Fatima, adding: "You probably think it's perfectly acceptable to leave all that to your wife and your cat."

Jaffa was just about to say that he'd never taken anyone else's belongings in his life, that he didn't have any daughters to forget to pick up from school and that Mona would be irate if he didn't do his fair share of the household tasks. But then he decided his best course of action was to stay silent.

"We're going to start your wonderful opportunity by using dream analysis," said Janina.

"Here, we take a structuralist perspective on dreams," Lily explained, smiling in what she hoped was a healing sort of way. "Who would like to start?"

Janina recounted her dream about Lenin. It did little to reassure the worried student.

"The dream world is part of the ideological superstructure of society influenced by the economic base, but it takes on a life of its own," explained Lily. "It has an internal logic that's part of the individual's biography. That individual's biography has been influenced by the society in which the dreamer has been brought up."

Jaffa nodded, trying to work out exactly what Lily meant.

"It's as if we're somewhere strange but it's as real as the physical world," said Fatima. "By wandering around in it, we find things out about ourselves. Dreams allow our hidden hopes and fears to dance."

At the word dance, Shaz jumped up. The session suddenly changed from dream analysis to dance therapy.

"The steps are not technically perfect," she said.

"They're improvisations, sometimes they repeat and sometimes they change," said Lily.

The women and amnesiacs started to dance around Jaffa, singing and humming. Perhaps because of his lack of sleep or perhaps because of the strange energy fields allegedly present in Lily's house, the local government officer found that he'd loosened his tie and was joining in.

After the dancing, the women helped Jaffa to externalise his emotions by creating an artefact made from his own choices of raw materials. The resources included: foil, coloured glass, buttons, string and cut out texts, photos and pictures.

Jaffa decided to make a tie pin. His grandfather had always worn one and he'd never owned one himself. He was so pleased with the finished result that he pinned it straight onto his tie.

Just as the women were about to show him how their teaching could provide him with a less exploitative attitude to women and divert him into a friendlier approach to planning, he suddenly remembered that he was supposed to be presenting an important document to a cross-party working group in Committee Room 30, and made a run for the door.

Lily, in hot pursuit, gave the prisoner a soft whack on the head with a trailing sub-tropical creeper, which was winding its way along the carpet. At this point, Jaffa remembered a second fact, which the unexpected events of the day had previously made him forget. He instantly vanished. One minute he was grappling with the door handle and being whacked over the head with lush foliage and the next he was gone. If the deputy director of planning had spent a whole year developing exit strategies, he couldn't have staged a more spectacular one. He had disappeared into thin air.

36

"The only thing worse than living with a woman who talks to a spider," said Owen to himself, "is living with a woman who talks to a dead spider."

He looked again at the note Janina had left him.

Gone to the forest. Sheep's head stew in oven.

Owen read the message twice, breathed deeply several times and wondered whether he should go and consult Dr Jelf about Janina's recent behaviour. He remembered that the last time he'd seen the doctor she'd been very dismissive and rude. He also remembered her consulting room with its safety hazards and decided to avoid it. He screwed the message up, unscrewed it and read it again. He put it in the bin, then he took it out, screwed it back up and threw it into the bin from varying angles. He did this by approaching the waste basket from different directions and throwing from alternative heights. After this, he re-read the contents of the note as if this procedure might have changed the message into something more comprehensible. It hadn't, so he changed his socks instead.

As a last resort Owen went to the bathroom to confide in Gladys, but Gladys wasn't there.

It was just after Jaffa's strange disappearance that Gertie Gupta arrived with some of the members of the Asian women's group. She was accompanied by Zosia with her midnight blue nails. Janina had contacted Gertie in case the sewing class members were interested in contributing to Jaffa's learning programme with their banners. Gertie and the women had been only too pleased to give their hard work a public airing. Unfazed by the fact that their first captive audience had escaped to freedom, they carried out a practice demonstration, chanting the slogans in three different languages.

Shaz decided to go back to work and find out what had happened to their escaped trainee. There had been a resurgence of heat. The weather had been slightly cooler for a few days but now the sun was back with a vengeance. The afternoon was blistering and Shaz squinted at the overexposed urban landscape as she drove to City Hall.

It was cool inside City Hall, the beautiful cream and green Victorian tiled corridors forming a civic Thermos flask.

It was eerily quiet. Only the sound of Shaz's stilettos clacking down the polished floors and a trail of perfume disturbed the stale air behind her. Shaz tap tapped through the maze-like intestines of the building. The large wooden door with the number 1033 and the word 'Planning' on it was on the third floor. Shaz pushed the door open and teetered in. She half expected something dramatic – like a completely empty space or Lily's forest. But the reality was disappointing. There was a yet smaller corridor with another set of doors. Hanging on the wall was a heavily framed photo of a Victorian looking man in a top hat. The shot was taken outdoors and the man had a spade in his hand. It was labelled: "Eli Sanderson, Chief Town Planner 1873-1892.". The door to the left had another number and name strip: 203, Jaffa Troy, Deputy Director of Planning. Shaz knocked on the door and swung it open without waiting for a reply.

Jaffa was sitting partly obscured, but not fully hidden, by his computer screen and a pile of papers, reading a book called *How to Become Invisible in Three Thousand Easy Steps*.

Shaz stared for a moment.

"Come in," said Jaffa, belatedly, in an effort to appear to be in control. He snapped his book on invisibility shut and placed it hurriedly on top of another entitled *Astral Projection: How to Free Up Your Life*. Then, as a hasty afterthought, he completed the tower with a conveniently concealing tome on urban planning. It was too large for the books beneath it. The whole structure swayed for a moment and then fell noisily to the floor.

"Why do I have a funny feeling that this might explain rather a lot?" said Shaz, intrigued, as she perched on a two-drawer filing cabinet after picking up the book.

Jaffa Troy examined the row of mouldy cups on his desk and gazed at the tie pin he'd made that morning, which was now between a photo of Mona and a strange object she'd made for him when she'd participated in a short pottery course. He decided he'd rather enjoyed his re-education programme once he'd got into it, and as Shaz looked as if she'd no intention of leaving, he decided he might as well tell her the truth.

"I'm only up to chapter three," he said. "It recommends sitting in a dark cupboard visualising your invisibility for hours on end and I've not had much time for that. Mona wants the whole of the downstairs redecorated before our wedding anniversary in October."

"I can see how the decorating could slow the process down," said Shaz.

"Though the astral projection helps," said Jaffa.

"The what?" asked Shaz.

"I started dabbling in it decades ago, in the nineties," said Jaffa, who was starting to enjoy telling her the story. He'd not mentioned anything to Mona in case she got both him and his astral projection decorating at the same time. "There were so many boring meetings to go to in the daytime and so many raves going on at night. I'd be up all night and then come into work and nearly fall asleep."

"So?" said Shaz.

"I thought that if I could master astral projection, I could send my astrally projected self into work while I slept at home. I gave up the late nights years ago but now I send my projection into work while I'm at home sanding down doors and stripping wallpaper."

"No wonder you were acting so strangely," said Shaz. "I thought you were leering at me, but you must have been in an astral trance."

"It's difficult maintaining the astral projection for a long time. I can't fully concentrate sometimes, especially when the DIY gets a bit involved. It's OK if I'm painting but when I'm wallpapering I can only half remember what my astral projection did the day before."

"You stole my ideas and put them forward as your own," said Shaz.

"The report on underpasses and pavements?" asked Jaffa. "I thought all the ideas came to me surprisingly quickly. I must have had a meeting with you while astral projecting. I forgot the meeting but retained the ideas."

Jaffa and Shaz both looked uncomfortable.

"Obviously I'll make sure that all the ideas are reattributed to you," said Jaffa.

"I have lots more good ideas," said Shaz. "We could do something about them."

"I've got a few myself," said Jaffa. "But things are discussed for so long that by the time something actually happens everyone's forgotten what it was they wanted to do in the first place."

"We could shake this place up," said Shaz.

"We could start by changing that dreary music the public have to listen to while they're on hold," said Jaffa.

"Good thinking," said Shaz.

"Let's get to work," said Jaffa, with an enthusiasm he hadn't felt for years.

Within half an hour, Shaz had called some friends and, by the time Lily phoned to see how they were going, "Greensleeves" had been replaced by an invigorating fusion of Arabic hip-hop and vintage bossa nova.

37

Robert and Owen stood next to the apple trees admiring the rate at which the fruit had grown in only a few days. The apples had expanded to their full extent like tart balloons, their waxy green skins almost ready to pop. Their stalks strained against the branches of the tree and a wasp already feasted on two that had broken free and thudded open on the ground, mushy explosions of natural sucrose now turning brown.

"Perhaps Janina would like some to make an apple crumble," said Robert. The words hung halfway between statement and question – a grammatical ambiguity. Both Owen and Robert knew that Janina wasn't the sort of woman who made apple crumbles very often.

"I'll get a carrier bag from the kitchen," said Owen.

Robert absentmindedly picked up a snail that was laboriously journeying up the trunk of the tree. He examined it closely for a few seconds and then put it in the plastic bowl ready to be deposited at nightfall on the grass verge at the bottom of the path that ran along the back of the street.

"We'll soon see the last of you," he said, after he'd found a space for it amongst the collection of other snails he'd gathered during the day. Each snail made its own track towards attempted freedom. Membership to the phylum *mollusca*, and an unexplained spot of midnight blue on the upper spiral of their shells, united them in common circumstance.

"We're going home in a few minutes," Owen told the girls, who were playing schools in the garden shed. He surveyed his father-in-law as he made his way back to him with the plastic bag. He felt rather sorry for Robert, a dispossessed man from another generation with no skills for maintaining the nuts and bolts of his emotional relationships.

"They don't have to be cooked," said Robert, as he filled the small carrier bag with fruit. "They can be eaten straight off the tree, though I find them slightly sour."

Owen took the bag and called the girls.

"Yuk," said Eve, after extracting an apple from the carrier bag and taking a small bite. She tossed the apple onto the grass, where it rolled and then settled at the side of the washing up bowl.

Robert raised an arm to acknowledge his son-in-law's and granddaughters' departure then picked up the plastic bowl. As he made his way down the footpath, he wondered whether Zosia would have changed in some way when she came back. Could she be a different woman altogether? He unloaded the snails onto the grass. The evening light was seeping away slowly through the cracks between houses, crawling over chimneys, and receding down moss-choked gutters. Aperture closing, the day had clicked onto automatic rewind to nightfall.

"Smile," said Zosia, sitting with her daughter and some of her new friends, enjoying a meal on the edge of Lily's forest and finishing off the last few exposures on the old-school roll of film she'd taken on her trip to India. The air was just starting to cool as twilight slid down the warm bark of the sheltering trees and mingled with the heat of the creeper-lined earth.

Although Jaffa Troy's capture hadn't gone without hitch, it had, nevertheless, ended as a success, so celebration was in the air. The sounds of knives and forks on plates and the chatter of friends intermeshed with the rustle of leaves and the call of birds. A wall-hanging of the forest scene, which Zosia had started embroidering, lay over the back of a chair and the conversation flitted like a colourful equatorial butterfly from one idea to another.

Zosia had told the amnesiacs that fruit was a wonderful aid to improving the memory. She'd written a thesis on the subject fifty years earlier, though it had never received the interest and acclaim it should have done. As a result of this timely snippet of information, the amnesia sufferers were eating a feast of tropical and temperate fruits served in delicious sauces.

"A few more days on a diet like this and you'll all be publishing your memoirs," said Shaz.

"From previous lives as well," said Monica.

"The interesting thing about eating food you've never eaten before is that you don't know which bits to eat first and which to leave until last because you don't know which bits you like best before you start eating them," said Lily.

"People often make very considered and wise choices about food yet very ill-considered decisions about their romantic relationships," said Zosia.

"I couldn't agree more," said Monica. "Both literature and real life are full of foolish heroines who make the most disastrous choices in men."

"But in some ways foolishness is a good thing," laughed Lily. "Foolishness implies the chance to make mistakes, and mistakes can only be made when we have the freedom to make poor judgements."

Janina's thoughts turned to Owen and, suddenly feeling unaccustomed guilt, she decided to go home.

Owen was in the kitchen pouring a cup of coffee from the cafetiere as Janina walked in. She poured herself a cup and added a spoon of brown sugar.

"Where are all those from?" she asked, seeing a pile of large green apples spilling out of a carrier bag.

"From Robert's tree," said Owen. "They're to make an apple crumble."

"I didn't know you knew how," said Janina.

She sat down with her coffee at the breakfast bar and decided to spend half an hour on a translation.

"There was something you said the other day that I didn't understand," said Owen. "I thought maybe we ought to clear it up."

Janina nodded absentmindedly, her thoughts already being drawn into the scientific thinking processes behind what the writer had expressed.

"The other Saturday morning when I had to work, you were half asleep and I thought you said something about … necrophilia," said Owen.

"I don't understand what you mean," Janina said, double-checking the soundness of the scientific logic presented in the paper while translating the words from Czech to English.

Owen swilled out his empty coffee cup and tried one of the apples. He decided that Robert and Eve were right, they were rather too tart to eat uncooked. He transferred the apples from the carrier bag into a basket where they would gradually become soft and mouldy waiting for someone to peel and chop them and put them in a saucepan. Janina would eventually identify the type of mould and then put them in the bin. He went upstairs. He sighed, popped four of Dr Jelf's pills into his mouth and crunched them slowly. The bottle looked half-empty although these were the first ones he'd taken.

Later, both Janina and Owen found themselves thinking about necrophilia, though from very different angles. Owen was wondering whether Janina's unexpected outburst was an attack on his own sexual finesse and that she'd meant that sleeping with him was like sleeping with a dead person. Janina, although she'd got into bed 45 minutes later than Owen, was already half asleep. She was thinking about the subject from Alexandra's point of view and wondering what witty retort she might make to Lenin. If she and Lenin had both been alive at the same time then, surely, Alexandra herself must also be dead. If two dead people had sex together was it still necrophilia? Or did that make it just regular dead sex? Janina muttered these two questions aloud but, fortunately, Owen was unable to make out what she was saying.

In Lily's forest, Shaz snored gently in her hammock in the guava trees. Like Zosia's embroidery, the forest fell soft and dark against the night in thick, uneven folds. Václav Havel yawned and stretched amongst a patch of sage and Zosia tiptoed furtively beneath the trees back to the house, a large collection of empty midnight blue nail varnish bottles clinking in her hands. A peacock called, a twig snapped and two dark shapes that might or might not have been small crocodiles slipped into the stream that wound its way through the trees.

Jaffa Troy was dreaming of dancing a rumba with Mona under a hot desert sky. Although in waking life he wouldn't have been sure what a rumba was, in the dream it involved a lot of dancing cheek to cheek, intense eye contact, swivelling about and Mona not talking about diets, dust or decorating. A cloud of earth kicked up from the dry ground obscured their complicated steps, avoiding any need for imagined choreography. As Jaffa Troy rumba'd through the gently contoured terrain of his subconscious, he noticed the dust thrown up from his and Mona's shoes turn into swirls of sand. Unfortunately, Mona noticed too and abruptly ended their passionate dance so she could fetch a dustpan and brush. By the time she returned, they were of little use against the desert wind that was becoming more forceful by the minute.

38

The weather changed overnight, as if summer had taken a last sweaty sprint towards the line that divided the seasonal quarter from autumn and then jumped over it. The sudden rush and impact of the landing created such a disturbance in the air that a wind swept through the city. It shook the leaves from the branches while they were still green, circumventing the usual change of colour from green to gold. A dramatic new subsection had been added to nature's policy on seasonal change and it had been ratified, then implemented, all in one night with no consultation.

Shaz awoke in the early hours of the morning, her hammock buffeted by a breeze winding its way through the tree trunks. Her face was splattered with rain, bouncing through the layers of leaves above her. The wind had found its way inside her head, disturbing the stillness, awakening – with disquieting flurries – an unexpected need to have a look at the house she'd shared with her boyfriend.

She turned down offers from Lily, Fatima and No Spoons to come with her. It was something she needed to do alone. She decided to go by bus. It would be too easy to drive there. The journey by public transport would give her time to think and give weight to the expedition. The tortuous bus service, sporadic and delayed, would add the necessary trauma that the occasion merited. It wasn't a cold wind, as such, but the air movement had brought the temperature down a few degrees. The morning itself carried grains of sand, which covered the city like a peculiar yellow frost.

Shaz was familiar with the bus routes. She was acquainted with the invisible architecture of the public transport system; the virtual tunnels that wound their way around the city like a crumbling labyrinth laid conceptually over the urban sprawl. How easy it would be to get temporarily lost, ejected from a bus that refused to go further, stopping before its usual peak time terminus. How easy to be marooned at the wrong bus stop as tides of self-engrossed pedestrians ebbed and flowed around you.

The number 53 into the centre of town was packed with office staff and shop assistants travelling to their work places. Shaz held on tight as it lurched along its predestined path. She let the half-heard conversations of anonymous people wash over her, settling back into the enforced, but not altogether unlikeable, community spirit that the public transport system fostered. This feeling of urban camaraderie waned after she got off and had to wait half an hour for the next bus.

When the 47 arrived, it was less crowded and she was able to get a seat on the upper deck. From this height, she watched green-topped, pewter-bellied leaves torn from tall trees skitter crazily along the damp pavements where the thin layer of sand had now turned to a just perceptible sludge. As the bus neared Shaz's destination, she became less sure of why she was going. She rationed her intake of breath as if the swoops of air outside were filling her lungs with too much oxygen. Paper bags, like strange birds, flapped up through the air as high as second floor windows. Displaced objects were flung across the streets and wedged in unlikely places. The flotsam and rubbish of everyday life was being transformed into something almost extraordinary.

Once off the bus, Shaz approached the street with trepidation, her head lowered. She was bleary-eyed against the wind. What if her ex was there? Was she ready for a confrontation? When, half blinded by the wind and dust, she got to where she thought the house should be – it wasn't there. The whole building had disappeared, just as the contents had done a few weeks earlier. Discarded by its owners, had it allowed itself to be blown away along with empty plastic bags and yellow polystyrene takeaway containers? The houses on either side remained rooted to the spot.

Shaz walked down the path of the neighbouring house. It was smaller than she remembered and had a new front door. Myrta, who usually wandered about the street or sat on the porch, must have been driven inside by the wild weather, for there was no sign of her. When Shaz knocked, there was no response. She opened her bag and placed it on the step. She took out a sheet of paper and a pen and scribbled a note asking her neighbour to get in touch with her at Lily's. But before she could quite finish the message, or push it through the letterbox, a gust of wind grabbed the sheet from her fingers and bore it off down the street – a large albino leaf amongst the orange and green. As she watched it go, grabbing at hedges and colliding with lamp posts, she started to weigh up the facts and formulate a conclusion. Her boyfriend must have somehow removed the whole structure of the house as he had with the contents before it.

Outside her former home, which was actually a few doors down from where the disoriented and sand-blinded Shaz had the notepaper torn from her hand, Myrta, astonished and excited by the strange change in weather, was hiding beneath a hedge. Fur flattened and swallowing the wind in long forgotten kitten yelps, she caught sight of something rectangular and white and gave chase as it fluttered along the pavement. It was too fast for her and the note finally plastered itself against the jacket of a wind-propelled pedestrian careering at a strange angle across the street. The man grasped at the paper as it fluttered against him and Myrta dived under the hedge, waiting for the next unsuspecting object to blow towards her.

A traffic cone was jammed inside an overturned dustbin as Janina made her way to the Queen's Head. An empty crisp packet flattened itself to the side of her head. A plastic carrier bag fluttered from the handle as she pushed the door open. Janina froze halfway into the pub, not quite believing what she could see. Together, between a wooden seat and a table, as if the strange weather had dragged them from their separate paths and wedged them there, was her husband and Gertie Gupta.

Could windy weather blow not just disassociated objects together in sudden new embraces, but people as well? A number of empty glasses were gathered on the table, as if the two of them had been there for some time. They were leaning towards each other in self-contained intimacy. As far as Janina knew, Gertie and Owen had never met. She hadn't bothered to introduce them because they would have nothing in common. Yet now, here they were as cosy and overlapping as constituent parts of a Venn diagram. Janina stood for a moment in the blustery doorway watching them laugh, enveloped in a warm blanket of conspiracy. Then she let the wind pull her back onto the street, out the way she'd come.

39

Janina confided her suspicions that Owen might be having an affair to Gladys.

"What do you think I should do?" she asked her invisible dead kinswoman. But her urgent enquiry was met with an echoing silence. It was only then that Janina realised that Gladys was no longer there. She hadn't had a conversation with the dead spider for some time. She'd been in such a hurry to get to Lily's, and so immersed in the kidnapping of the deputy planning director, that she'd forgotten to invite Gladys along.

Actually, Gladys had been invited to the Queen's Head by Owen. He felt unable to discuss his relationship worries at work, his conversations with colleagues limited to discussions about the safest storage methods for hazardous chemicals and whether legislation should be changed on minimum and maximum temperature thresholds. Lunchtime discussions sometimes ricocheted into the subject of dogs, as two of his colleagues kept greyhounds, and now and then timorously branched out into the relatively unfamiliar territory of holidays. However, they never stretched as far as a discussion about their domestic circumstances. This would have been too wide a chasm for even Owen, as an experienced mountaineer, to leap.

Likewise, his conversations with his mountaineering buddies had set parameters. They ranged from practical considerations about climbing boots and equipment to heady talk of future climbs to difficult summits. Their conversations didn't involve the difficult north face of the emotional landscape.

In an effort to disperse the volatile mixture of emotions inside him before it reached a dangerously inflammable level, Owen had fallen into chatting to Gladys. Gladys, strangely, had taken on a physical existence again. She was large and black and a very good listener. To be honest, Owen had started chatting to her before he could see her but, when he'd opened the bathroom cabinet one day, she'd been sitting there as visible and substantial as Owen himself. Confiding in Gladys was Owen's first faltering step on a journey he knew he had to take to save his relationship with Janina. He suspected that Gladys was rather peeved by Janina's waning attention, so he'd decided to invite her out on a little trip to the pub.

After Gertie left, Owen and Gladys stayed to have a drink with Alex, and they were soon joined by Bill Gupta. Since Owen had introduced the strange subject of necrophilia into a conversation with Bill and Alex, the subject had become one of their set pieces. It didn't make an appearance quite as often as crocodiles, the monarchy, sausages and the price of beer but it was there as an unlikely topic in the unwritten list of options.

"I wonder if there are any links between necrophiliacs and cannibalism," said Alex, taking a crisp from a packet of cheese and onion offered around by Owen during a rather long lull in the conversation.

Gladys must have been glad that the conversation had taken this turn as it was a topic on which she was at least partly qualified to have an opinion. Although all her friends mated with their lovers while they were still alive, they didn't remain that way for very long afterwards.

"Sex and food should both be a celebration of life, not anything to do with the dead," said Bill, helping himself to another handful of crisps.

"Wakes," said Alex, "are a celebration of death, but finger food, alcohol and the reminder of your own mortality all encourage the urge for sex."

"Wakes aren't a celebration of death," said Bill. "They're to celebrate the dead person's life."

"And the dead person isn't involved in the drinking, eating or sex," said Owen.

The four of them took some time to think this over. A customer left, letting in a whoosh of sandy air and an assortment of madly dancing leaves.

"I wonder if they have crocodile sausages in Australia," said Alex, setting off on a different conversational tangent.

The whirling leaves came to a stop near Bill's feet, reminding him of an event that had happened earlier in the day. He felt in his pocket and took out a piece of paper that had blown onto him in the street when he'd popped back to his old house to collect the post. Myrta had been outside, chasing about like a crazy thing, and he'd changed his mind about crossing the road. He'd noticed that there was writing on the paper and he'd put it in his jacket pocket.

Please contact me urgently at 114 Wineberry Drive, it said in hasty forward slanting writing.

Bill screwed the paper up into a ball and put it back in his pocket. Meanwhile, in Owen's pocket, Gladys – not having much knowledge of either sausages or crocodiles – gave up on the conversation. She finished chewing one of Owen's tablets, which she'd become rather addicted to since discovering them spilling out of the bottle a few weeks earlier. She made herself comfortable and went to sleep.

The beer and vodka were starting to go to Owen's head. He'd not been sleeping well and was drinking on an empty stomach. He had an urge to unburden himself, to confide in another human rather than another species.

"I've got a spider in my pocket," he said tentatively to Bill.

"Have you?" said Bill. "I've got a hamster in mine."

It wasn't the reply Owen had expected. The two men looked at each other for a moment wondering what sort of society, what set of circumstances, and what chasms of misunderstanding between the sexes led grown men to carry small mammals and arachnids around in their pockets for company.

"They say," said Alex, "that the Queen has never ever eaten a sausage in the whole of her life."

The other two men crunched on the last of the cheese and onion crisps while weighing up this information.

"Not even venison sausages?" asked Bill.

"Not even venison ones," Alex confirmed.

Bill decided that he would do something adventurous for once in his life. He'd visit the address on the paper.

"Say there's three men in a pub having a conversation. Does that by definition make it 'men's talk'?" Shaz asked

Lily, Monica and Janina. "Or is 'men's talk' something more specific?"

Shaz had discovered the phenomenon of 'men's talk' when, after divorcing her first husband, she went out with her first post-marriage boyfriend. They'd slept in her boyfriend's rather cramped single bed. Lack of space had encouraged them to get up earlier than they otherwise might have done. It had been a drizzly early morning. They'd walked in the rain to the park and watched the rabbits and guinea pigs huddled in their enclosures. Then they'd hurried through the damp streets to the train station and had a cup of coffee and a beer in the café. While they were there, they'd bumped into her boyfriend's workmate and his girlfriend. The two men had wandered to the bar and Shaz had made to follow them.

"You can't follow them," the girl had said, grabbing Shaz's arm. "They're having a men's talk."

Shaz had never heard the expression 'men's talk' before. It sounded like something her ex-husband might have said. She felt that if it had to exist at all, it should have been assigned strictly to a period before the Second World War or, at the very least, not beyond the early 1960s. She wondered what it was. Later she'd wished that she'd had the presence of mind to ask the girl. But, presumably, if girls were never privy to these exchanges then she wouldn't have known either. She'd been left with the question lurking somewhere at the back of her mind.

"If we knew what it was maybe we'd be able to make some sense of what men do," said Shaz.

"Everything seemed so positive yesterday," said Lily. "And now Shaz's house has disappeared and Janina's husband is having an affair."

"It's not just any old affair," said Janina. "He's having an affair with my mother's friend who also happens to be the sister of my friend Bill – who I didn't have an affair with because I didn't want to upset my husband."

"I wonder what will happen next." said Lily, as Janina left to go home.

She turned half hopefully to Monica but, before Monica could throw any light on the future, there was a tremendous gust of wind that rocked the house. This was followed by an urgent knocking at the front door.

"Janina must have forgotten something," said Lily.

But when Lily opened the door there was a man standing on the step.

"Hello, Lily," he said. "It's me, your husband. I've come home."

40

The man on the doorstep's proclamation made Lily's heart sink, but only for a second because – despite his words – he didn't have Ernest's voice or, for that matter, his head. Although his clothes looked like her late husband's, the person inside them was definitely not the man to whom she'd been married. For a start, he was a good thirty or forty years younger than Ernest.

"You're certainly here," said Lily, resorting to logic to deal with the situation, "but you're not my husband and I'm afraid this isn't your home."

The man looked so downcast that Lily hurriedly invited him in. He sat forlornly in an armchair sipping a cup of tea with honey and sugar. Lily had thought he looked as if he could do with something both soothing and energising to drink.

"I woke up lying in the gutter one day and couldn't remember who I was," he said. "Everything was just a blank. All I had with me were the clothes on my back and a bag with some more clothes in it."

"What made you decide you were married to me?" asked Lily.

"I found a letter and a note in the pocket of the jacket I was wearing," said the man. "The note was from someone called Lily to someone called Ernest and the letter was from a friend of Ernest's and referred to Lily as Ernest's wife. Because I was wearing the clothes, I assumed that I was Ernest. So, I naturally believed that I lived at the address on the envelope and that you were my wife."

It was all starting to make sense to Lily. This man was another victim of the privatised ambulance service – yet another amnesia sufferer. He must have bought the clothes in a charity shop before losing his memory. She must have missed the note and the letter when she'd half-heartedly gone through the pockets of Ernest's clothes before taking them to the shop.

"This really is a lovely cup of tea," said the new amnesiac.

"Welcome, Honey Sugar," said Shaz.

"I think the clothes in the bag must be yours," the newly named Honey Sugar told Lily. "They're women's clothes in a dry cleaner's bag. But if I'm not your husband why was I picking them up from the dry cleaner's for you?"

Lily had a look inside the bag but she didn't recognise any of the contents. The dress was far more elegant than anything she would wear. The blouse was much more sophisticated and she'd never worn a beautiful auburn wig in her life. Although now she'd seen this one, she was rather tempted.

As they were mulling the situation over, there was another knock at the door. It was Bill Gupta. Incorrectly presuming that Bill was yet another person suffering from memory loss, Lily ushered him in before he could introduce himself. Václav Havel took one look at him, shivered and ran out of the room. Bill was surprised that a cat seemed so frightened of him when it was usually the other way round. Amelia the Second, who he'd brought along with him for moral support, had been peeping out of his jacket pocket, causing the nervous reaction in Václav. Lily, noticing the little hamster and her effect on the cat, remembered the dream she'd had about Václav.

"I came round because I found this note," said Bill.

He gently removed the piece of paper from beneath Amelia's feet and showed it to Lily.

"Where did you get that from?" asked Shaz, surprised.

"The wind blew it into my hand as if it was meant for me," said Bill. Shaz took the paper from him, wiping off a few grains of sand that still stuck to it. Bill looked strangely familiar to her. The day was getting stranger and stranger.

"I wrote it," she said.

"Why don't you two go for a walk?" suggested Monica, with the knowing look of a clairvoyant.

"Watch out if you go very far into the forest," said Lily, as Bill and Shaz wandered off together. "I thought I spotted a crocodile in there a few days ago."

Bill was more concerned about Václav Havel making a reappearance than any crocodiles, despite Alex's cousin's unpleasant experience. However, if Václav was anywhere in the forest, he was well hidden and Bill was feeling unusually at ease and confident. As he and Shaz pieced their stories together, and realised that they used to be neighbours, Bill wondered why he'd never noticed Shaz when she'd lived next door to him. Under the magical forest canopy, a mutual attraction bloomed like the starlight lustre of night flowering orchids. They exchanged their life stories. Bill ending his with rediscovering the note while he was in the pub.

"So, there were three of you? Three men having a conversation in the pub," stated Shaz. "Would you mind telling me what you were talking about?"

"I don't think it was very interesting," said Bill.

"Believe me, it would be a revelation," said Shaz.

"We talked about sausages," recalled Bill.

"Sausages?" said Shaz, incredulously.

"Venison sausages," said Bill.

Shaz's laughter woke up Amelia the Second and, sensing the emotional as well as thermal warmth, she decided she didn't want to be left out. She popped up out of Bill's pocket. Bill introduced her to Shaz.

"Amelia the First escaped," said Bill. "My landlady was really worried. She said she'd eat the house but of course she didn't."

Shaz stared at him.

"That's it!" she said. "She didn't eat your house because she tunnelled through the wall and ate mine instead."

41

"If I don't live here," Honey Sugar said to Lily. "Do you think I might live in that house in your garden?"

"There isn't a house in the garden," said Lily.

But that's where Lily was wrong.

It was a red brick house and Shaz and Bill had also just discovered it. There were three steps up to its blue front door, which had a brass knocker on it. Frida Kahlo was sitting contentedly on the top step washing her face. Shaz and Bill agreed that the house bore an uncanny resemblance to Shaz's. Intoxicated by new love, and a few of Lily's rum punches, it was perfectly clear to Shaz what had happened. Her former house had been eaten by Amelia the First and then regurgitated, all in one piece, in the forest at the edge of Lily's garden. Quite how Amelia the First had got there was harder to explain. Shaz guessed the hamster had stowed away in her handbag when she'd put it down on the neighbour's step to write the note. The house wasn't absolutely identical to Shaz's but travelling through the digestive tract of a hamster was bound to have altered it to some extent.

"How could a house be eaten by something as small as a hamster?" asked Fatima, who'd just arrived.

Only two things were certain: firstly, the house was undoubtedly there and, secondly, the planning department wouldn't like it.

"Let's ask Jaffa for his advice," said Shaz, "before the planning department gets to hear about it."

"It wasn't planned. It wasn't even built. It was eaten elsewhere and then regurgitated, without my permission, by a runaway hamster," Lily tried to explain to the chief planning officer on the phone the following day.

"It's still a serious infringement of the byelaws," the chief planning officer said, sitting up straighter at his desk and raising his eyebrows officiously at the deputy planning officer. But his deputy looked as if he'd gone into a trance.

"It's true, it is against the byelaws to have a house in your garden without planning permission," whispered Jaffa, who was really only a few feet away from Lily. "We need the help of a top legal expert."

"I'll make everyone a cup of tea," said Janina, who'd just arrived. She was surprised to find Bill there. She hadn't yet questioned him to find out if he knew about Owen's affair with Gertie. Janina had spent the night on the sofa. She'd had no chance to challenge Owen yet about his affair. He seemed to be in a drink-induced stupor.

There had been no waking him when she'd got home late the night before, or even in the morning. It wasn't like Owen to miss work. She called his line manager, telling him that Owen was unable to get out of bed. She said he had a sore throat and a very sore head, which Janina was sure was the truth. He'd wake with a terrible hangover. She could smell the alcohol from the bedroom doorway.

Honey Sugar had spent a reasonably comfortable night on the sofa bed at Lily's. He'd left his dry cleaner's bag on the floor, where Janina tripped over it on her way back with cups of tea, sending the contents of the bag spilling out.

Shaz had been gazing at Honey Sugar for some time wondering why he looked familiar. When she saw what was in the bag, she realised why.

"There's a legal expert in the room already," she said, picking up the wig and placing it on the newest amnesia sufferer's head.

"I know who you are," she said. "You're Bryan."

Bryan was one of the men Shaz had interviewed in her research into transvestites. She hadn't recognised him at first in his boringly conventional attire. He was highly regarded in the local community and punctilious in raising gender issues amongst the wider population. Shaz also knew that Bryan was an eminent lawyer. His forte was using ancient byelaws to fight the inconsistencies of the modern legal system, ensuring that justice was done where justice was deserved. Shaz knew his address, so Fatima offered to give him a lift home. Once back in his flat, he could pore over ancient law books to help Lily out of her predicament.

Janina decided she'd better go home and see if Owen had woken up. A number of large trees lay in Lily's garden, blown down by the ferocious and unexpected wind that had abated as suddenly as it had started. It was quite possible, Janina thought, that the house in Lily's garden had been there for a long time, shielded from view by the thick foliage of the trees. She knew there'd been a plan to build a housing development in that part of the park a few years ago. It had been vetoed in the end and there'd been accusations of corruption amongst some of the councillors. One of them had fled the country to avoid prosecution. There'd been some talk of building having started even though permission hadn't been given. This house could drag up old inter-party battles and be a huge embarrassment to the local authority unless it was kept quiet. But Janina had other things on her mind so, instead of going back to ask the others if this was actually a more plausible scenario for the house's sudden appearance, she went home.

As she turned into her street, she noticed two figures getting into a car parked outside her home. Even from that distance, she was able to see that the figures were Gertie and Zosia. For a moment Janina felt puzzled, then she felt angry, then she felt as if she was going to cry. How could Gertie have the nerve to come round to her home? And why was Zosia, her own mother, condoning such a thing? She pulled in as the other car drove off. She sat for some time thinking or trying not to think at all.

Owen was sitting, smiling nervously, in the living room. He was cleaning his climbing boots. He nodded his head at two things that were placed on the table. One was a bouquet of flowers and the other was an envelope addressed to Janina. It was propped against a vase in which Owen had placed the flowers. Janina remembered hearing that men sometimes bought flowers when they felt guilty.

Bryan Honey Sugar, as he had now become known, spent all day sifting through his books. His brilliant mind and his expertise in the law helped him to find and then weld together ancient pieces of long-forgotten legislation. In no time at all, he'd created a brilliant and watertight defence for Lily. His argument was involved and complex. It was expressed in legalese so that neither Lily nor her friends understood most of it. However, they did grasp that it made use of an ancient byelaw protecting the grazing rights of animals and another byelaw protecting the rights of property owners to the waste products emitted by animals on their land. The first piece of legislation had un-doubtedly been written more with the grazing of sheep and cows in mind than feral hamsters, and the second more with manure in mind than regurgitated houses. Neverthe-less, by the time Bryan Honey Sugar had finished, he had the council in a tight spot. Lily was out of trouble and Shaz had her house back – even if it was in a different location and rather altered in appearance.

When Robert took his granddaughters home that evening, they were all surprised to find Owen and Janina smiling and talking to each other.

"You wouldn't listen to anything I had to say anymore," Owen had told Janina, "and gave all your attention to your translations. The only way I could think of to get your attention and make amends was to have my words translated into Polish and Hindi. I contracted Professor Kaminski and Miss Gupta to do the work. I did try to find an Ancient Arabic translator as well, but you seem to have cornered the market on that one."

Janina had read the translations. In them, he promised to do his fair share of the housework and to never ever forget to pick up the children from school. The letter even included some scientific formulas and mathematical drawings, expressing Owen's feelings for her. If Janina had wanted to be picky, she could have questioned Owen's use of some of the symbols but she found she didn't wish to be picky. She could see that the emotions behind the expressions were deeply felt if not mathematically robust or deployed in a strictly conventional way. The formula she liked best just stated:

$$\text{Janina} + \text{Owen} = \heartsuit^{\nearrow} \qquad \underline{T} \ \} \ O + J = \odot$$

$$\overline{}$$

$$\dagger \qquad O - J = \text{☁}$$

The use of the 'always true' symbol and the one depicting indivisibility could not be said to be elegant but, nestled beside the pictograms, they were rather joyous. For a moment Janina wondered if she should reciprocate by expressing her own newly recovered feelings for Owen in the form of a written health and safety protocol. Thankfully, the moment was fleeting.

That night Janina dreamt of Lenin and Alexandra once more.

"Fuck all this Leninism and necrophilia crap," said Alexandra. "Let's live a little."

"Let's climb a mountain," said Lenin. "And do a translation together on the summit, then go home and have some of your delicious sheep's head stew."

"You're on," said Alexandra. "Maybe we should have a few friends round. We could invite Martov and those Mensheviks, they're probably not such a bad lot when you get to know them."

"Fine by me," said Lenin. "But don't invite Joe."

"Who?" asked Alexandra.

"That Stalin guy with the silly moustache," said Lenin.

"He's the kind of man who gives totalitarianism a bad name," said Alexandra.

"That's a good thing, isn't it?" pondered Lenin.

"I suppose it is," said Alexandra.

"Does that mean we have to invite him after all?" asked Lenin.

"No," said Alexandra, after only a moment's thought. "We'll already have enough guests. One sheep's head can only make so much stew."

42

The hungry pink mouth of a new day mewed into existence. Kitten soft, it crept over the rooftops like creamy milk from a tipped jug. It trickled into windows, innocently nudging alarm clocks into motion. Its sleek sides wound around the poles of rotary washing lines. Creaking into motion, the invisible cranks and pulleys hoisting back the remnants of night. The inhabitants of the city lay in bed, squeezing tranquillity from the last few moments of half-sleep. They sifted their fantasies from reality, rolled out from the cocoon of warm bedding, leaving the residue of their dreams huddled safely amongst the creases in the sheets and the rivulets of the duvet. They weighed up the choices for the day, what fortune had in store. Only reality accompanied their bare feet onto the cold tiles of the bathroom floor.

Yet change was in the air, borne on a sand-bearing wind. Lily felt it as she dressed. The city council would soon click its castanets to the flamenco rhythm of its telephone system. The tea ladies in City Hall would sing arias in Italian and Portuguese as they pushed the first of many tea trolleys along the cream tiled corridors. The traffic regulation systems, subways, school corridors, dockland redevelopment designs, and payroll division would all respond to the beat. The ambulance service contract would be won by a not-for-profit voluntary sector organisation and the joyriding ambulances would come to a confused stop. Their redeemed and re-trained drivers would drive on roadways instead of over pavements. Even the speeches and brain waves of the party leaders would be syncopating to the new rhythm.

When Lily went downstairs, Frida Kahlo was waiting patiently for breakfast but Václav Havel was nowhere to be seen. Lily hadn't set eyes on him since he'd caught sight of Amelia the Second. She had a feeling he'd disappeared back to wherever he'd come from.

Happily, the amnesiacs' memories had miraculously reappeared. Dr Jelf checked them out before they went their separate ways. After all, the fact that they'd been in an ambulance suggested they'd been ill. But Dr Jelf could find nothing wrong with them. Perhaps the high fruit diet that had helped bring their memories back had also improved their general health. The sub-tropical climate might have also played a part in their restoration, along with the soothing but stimulating atmosphere of Lily's house.

"Those tablets you gave Owen did the trick," Janina told Celia Jelf.

"They were placebos," said Celia. "I prescribed them more for your benefit than his."

"Well, be careful who you prescribe them to because they work," said Janina. "You should have seen what they did for my late grandmother. I told you that things are more complicated than you think."

"Did your hand really pass through Owen's arm?" asked Celia.

"Truth is always much more complicated than surface appearances," said Janina. "I was inhabiting an existence that was detached from the one Owen occupied. We lived in separate spaces that were merely superimposed."

"I've been mulling over that conversation we had," Celia said. "And I've decided to quit the GP foothills and set off in a different direction."

"Up the male hierarchy?" asked Janina.

"No, I'm going into medical philosophy," said Celia, "working on a thesis called *The Links Between Metaphors and Matter in the Human Mind*."

"Honestly," said Janina. "You don't have to get a PhD just to win an argument."

Monica Moule carried on reading with renewed enthusiasm. In a literary journal she subscribed to, she read an interesting article about Václav Havel. She forwarded it to Lily. It said that the manuscript of a previously unknown play written by the late president had recently been discovered. Unusually, the play featured Václav himself, and in line with one strand of Czech tradition, he was metamorphosed into the form of another creature – in this case, something a little more furry and domesticated than an insect.

Monica had lots of stories to tell Marlene and carried on with her tea cup readings. Although the readings often revealed amazing things, Monica no longer saw any reason to disbelieve them.

Gladys, like Václav Havel, had also disappeared. Owen's tablets were all gone too. Perhaps she'd decided to search for more to retain her newly regained physical presence.

Electric shocks of happiness startled their way through Shaz and Bill Gupta's lives. They both ached physically and emotionally with love. It was the sort of ache you experience in your jaw when you laugh for too long or when, as a child, you chewed a never-ending liquorice shoelace. Except this added a metaphorical shine to their teeth so that every time they looked in the mirror and smiled, they remembered why they were happy. It was a feeling that even the fluoride added to the city's water supply couldn't remove.

The parks department, helped by a team of enthusiasts – including Lily and some of her new friends – reclaimed the area around Shaz's house as a tropical and sub-tropical arboretum. It was rumoured that a number of potentially dangerous animals had been found and thoughtfully repatriated to warmer climates.

Shaz and Jaffa continued to carry out innovative work within the city council and often had tea breaks together although, as Jaffa progressed through his book on invisibility, Shaz wasn't always sure whether he was there or not. Mona continued her mission to establish the first ever totally dust-free environment and stopped attending the Calories Club. She started to get more exercise by helping in the tropical arboretum instead.

The day after Owen presented Janina with the translations, Zosia was standing in her back garden watching Robert putting snails back on the apple trees.

"There are 80,000 species of snail," said Zosia.

"Some of these are very unusual," said Robert. "They have a spot of blue on their shell."

"Perhaps that's 80,001 species then," said Zosia. "New species appear all the time, adjusting to new circumstances. Although these ones may have been helped a little in the interests of scientific research."

Robert straightened up and looked at the expanse of garden leading back to the kitchen.

"You've not told me anything about your trip to India yet," he said.

They walked towards the house, tentatively arm in arm like new lovers, stepping across the familiar green turf to somewhere new.

That same day, Janina and Owen had decided to make the most of the early autumn sunshine and had driven to the seaside with the girls. It was cooler at the coast as they leant over the promenade railings looking at the sea. Winter was almost visibly advancing in the grey waves. They braced themselves, half enjoying the coldness of the spray and half enduring it, staying just long enough to make the journey worthwhile.

"You might have told me you wanted to call our daughter Eve so that her name would spell Everest," said Janina. "I had no idea until Professor Kaminski pointed it out."

"That's an ingenious notion. But it's not why I chose it," said Owen. "I liked the name because my great-grandmother was called Eve. The mountain connection is one of Professor Kaminski's own imaginings."

Turning away from the cold expanse of water, Janina tried to imagine Professor Kaminski having imaginings. Perhaps everyone did and they just didn't talk about them.

Elsewhere, Celia Jelf was planning her research and asking

Gladys her opinion, while Fatima was frantically writing a story that was nearing its end.

Thousands of miles away, two crocodiles slipped into a warm sea – the small spot of midnight blue nail polish on their backs almost indistinguishable in the dusky light. They disappeared beneath the paler blue of the waves, noses pointing back to the familiarity of cooler climes. Homeward.

Acknowledgements

A huge thank you to Jo Haywood, my amazing editor at Valley Press who's helped *Foolish Heroines* emerge as clear and lustrous as it can be. Thanks also to the Blue Pencil Agency for longlisting this book for the BPA First Novel Award.

Thanks to Linda Snell, Marilyn Francis, Christiane Glennie, Jane Dezonie and Celia Jenkins for their writerly support and friendship. Life would be less rich without their co-critiquing and coffee chats.

Thanks also to my friends in Bath Writers and Artists, especially Sue Boyle for organising us (not an easy or enviable task).

I also extend my thanks to Good Fortune for my going to school before strange and unforgivable things were done to the English syllabus. Thanks to South Hunsley School, especially my English teachers: John Roberts, Brian Spencer and Bryan Gardner, who were always inspiring. Also, my tutors on the Creative Writing MA at Bath Spa University, Mimi Thebo and Tessa Hadley.

To my family: Nick, Lucia, Louise, Onur, James, Niamh, Jamie, Daniel and Leo. You all bring happiness to my life (and sometimes fish and chips, cake and beer).

Thanks to my mum, my dad, my brother Jim and my nana and grandpa. I lost you all when I was far, far too young. You taught me that reading, writing, imagination, wonder, kindness and humour are all essentials of life.

Thanks to the city of Hull and the East Riding of Yorkshire. Your minerals are the bedrock of my bones and your geography and poetry are laid down in my soul.

To the parks and libraries of my life, particularly East Park, Hull and Hull Central Library but also Heaton Park, Manchester and the parks and libraries of Bristol and Bath and this little corner of Wiltshire.

More debatably, I must not forget to mention Ethel. And, as cats have padded their quiet trails and trackways through the novel, it would be careless of me not to mention the cats that have shared my own life: Kitty, Prue, Claudius and Figaro. How tempting it is to allow these acknowledgements to metamorphose into a feral litter of cat biographies but I must resist.

Finally, thank you to other magic realist writers past and contemporary: Nikolai Gogol, Franz Kafka, Flann O'Brien, Louis de Bernières, Haruki Murakami and Monique Roffey, to name just a few. Their literary worlds have beguiled me and assured me that writing magical realism is not an affliction but something wise and wonderful.